Help! Someone Help Me!

But why did she need help? she wondered. Pressure built and thrust its way into her lungs until her cry came out a sob. She forced her eyes open. At first, she couldn't control her vision. But then she saw an outline of a man. She recognized him, yet she didn't.

"Stephanie?"

Who was that? Was he talking to her? If so, she didn't recognize that name.

The tall, lean man was still there. A plastic bandage covered one eyebrow, and his features were drawn and pinched. Stephanie resisted the urge to give in to panic. Instead, she forced herself to speak. "Yes... I can hear you. But who's—who's Stephanie? She watched as the lines in his forehead deepened, forcing his eyebrows to point toward the center.

"You're Stephanie," he said. "Stephanie Marsh."

Dear Reader,

Happy summertime reading from all of us here at Silhouette! As the days of summer wind to an end, take the time to curl up with August's wonderful love stories. These are books as hot as the most sizzling summer's day!

We start with Mary Lynn Baxter's *Man of the Month* novel *Tall in the Saddle,* which has a hero you'll never forget—Flint Carson, a man as rugged and untamed as the land he ranches. This is a book you'll want to read over and over again. It's a keeper!

Also in August comes a wild, witty romp from Lass Small, *The Molly Q.* Don't ask me to explain; I'll just say it has to do with computers, kidnapping and marvelous fun.

Rounding out August is *A Wolf in Sheep's Clothing,* a tie-in to July's *Never Tease a Wolf*—both by the talented Joan Johnston. And don't miss books from Naomi Horton, Ryanne Corey and Sally Goldenbaum. Each and every Silhouette Desire novel this month is one that I am keeping in my personal library.

So go wild with Desire—you'll be glad you did.

All the best,

Lucia Macro
Senior Editor

MARY LYNN BAXTER

TALL IN THE SADDLE

SILHOUETTE *Desire*®

Published by Silhouette Books New York

America's Publisher of Contemporary Romance

 SILHOUETTE BOOKS
300 East 42nd St., New York, N.Y. 10017

TALL IN THE SADDLE

ISBN: 0-373-05660-5

First Silhouette Books printing August 1991

Printed in the U.S.A.

Books by Mary Lynn Baxter

Silhouette Intimate Moments

Another Kind of Love #19
Memories that Linger #52
Everything but Time #74
A Handful of Heaven #117
Price Above Rubies #130
When We Touch #156
Fool's Music #197
Moonbeams Aplenty #217
Knight Sparks #272
Wish Giver #296

Silhouette Desire

Shared Moments #24
Added Delight #527
Winter Heat #542
Slow Burn #571
Tall in the Saddle #660

Silhouette Special Edition

All Our Tomorrows #9
Tears of Yesterday #31
Autumn Awakening #96
Between the Raindrops #360

MARY LYNN BAXTER

sold hundreds of romances before she ever wrote one. The D & B Bookstore, right on the main drag in Lufkin, Texas, is her home as well as the store she owns and manages. She and her husband, Leonard, garden in their spare time. Around five o'clock every evening, they can be found picking butter beans on their small farm just outside of town.

Special thanks to Troy Hill for all of his help

One

From afar a baby screamed. Closer, two teenagers exchanged a passionate kiss. A bored voice droned over the intercom, announcing flight information.

Flint Carson paid scant attention to the sights and sounds around him. He was too intent on making his way through the airport concourse in Little Rock, Arkansas. For the first time in months, if not years, there was a spring to his gait.

Hours in the saddle and manual labor had supplied him with a wealth of energy, yet his movements were economical and purposeful. He never seemed in a hurry. At six foot three, he towered over the average citizen. His weight was adequate where it ought to be; life had given him a lean hardness.

Thank God, the trip to the Diamond A Ranch had paid off, he thought. He'd gotten confirmation that he was on the right track with his breeding of the Brahngus cattle. He was hell-bent on building them into a profitable herd.

And to think he hadn't wanted to make the trip. Flint had felt he couldn't be away from his struggling ranch in East Texas for a day, much less several. But if he were to crossbreed any more stock, he'd have no choice, especially with money being in such short supply. With no guarantees, he'd already used what little cash he had.

"Hey, mister, watch where you're goin', will ya?"

Flint paused, realizing he'd unconsciously sideswiped a fellow passenger with his duffel bag. "Sorry," he muttered.

The man glowered at him. "Yeah, me, too."

For an instant Flint felt himself bristle, but then sound judgment took over and he merely shrugged, turned his back and walked off. One smart-mouth kook wasn't worth getting riled over. He didn't stop again until he'd reached the gate that posted his Houston flight.

He dropped his duffel bag in a deserted corner and leaned against the wall. But it was almost impossible for him to remain idle. Impatiently he removed his Stetson hat and ran his hand through his thick chestnut-colored hair. When that gesture failed to calm his restlessness, he shoved the hat back on his head and let his thoughts wander back to his project.

This Brahngus line could be the break he'd been waiting for. Even at that, he couldn't allow himself to get too excited or optimistic. He'd failed at so much lately. In fact, failure had been such a part of his life that he'd gotten used to it, like an old pair of boots.

Flint had never known complete security or lasting solace. So he had a habit of accepting the brief moments of comfort as exactly that—brief. As a precaution against the anxiety, chaos and defeat he knew were sure to follow, he readied himself.

Flint had found out at an early age that life was not fair, that only the tough survived. A change-of-life baby, he'd been neglected more often than not. His mother had been lazy, and his daddy had worked all the time. Yet money had always been scarce.

His daddy had hounded him to go to work as soon as he was old enough, but Flint had wanted to participate in school sports. Somehow he'd managed to juggle both successfully. In the end, sports had been his salvation. They'd gotten him a college scholarship.

During his college years, Flint had developed a fascination with law enforcement and worked toward making that a career. He'd also worked at overcoming the shock and loss of his parents. They were killed when a tornado ripped through their mobile home.

Upon graduation Flint had gone to work for the Houston Police Department. He'd been recruited by the Drug Enforcement Agency after special training and had worked there until a drug bust went sour and he was injured, forcing him into a leave of absence.

But dredging up thoughts of his ill-fated childhood and perils on the job was a waste of time and good energy. The problems he faced now had nothing to do with the past. The way he looked at it, he'd been given a clean slate, and he aimed to make the best of it or die trying.

The overhead intercom screeched in Flint's ear. He frowned and at the same time reached for a cigarette only to remember with disgust that he'd given up the nasty habit months ago. He settled for a piece of gum while his eyes wandered around the waiting area. It teemed with people of all sizes, ages and nationalities. Instead of being fascinated, he was repulsed. He hated crowded flights. He hated crowds period. Give him the wide open spaces and his privacy anytime.

Only after Flint slapped his pocket again and looked back up did he see her. A woman, who looked to be in her late twenties, was laughing at something someone was saying to her. She was in his direct line of vision, and for a moment Flint was held by the sound of her husky laughter.

She was a real looker to boot. Her milk-white skin and gently curving mouth were perfect foils for curly black hair that framed her face and shone like black silk. And she had the body to match the face. She was dressed in an off-white suit. Her blouse was silk and her high, firm breasts molded the soft fabric in a way that confirmed his guess that she didn't have on a bra.

He turned his gaze, but not before shifting uncomfortably. He fared no better, however, when he concentrated on her legs. They seemed endless. And her derriere was round and tight.

"Damn," he muttered, then slapped his empty pocket again for a cigarette, all without taking his eyes off her. It wasn't so much her beauty that mesmerized Flint, as it was her total unawareness of it. Or, he corrected himself, her calm acceptance of it as a God-given right.

Again he realized he was staring, and cursed vehemently. Still, he didn't turn away, watching as a stocky, sour-faced man approached her. If her reaction was anything to judge by, she wasn't glad to see him. Her face lost its color, and her mouth tightened into a straight line.

His curiosity more than a little aroused, Flint propped a booted foot against the wall and watched as the man closed the distance between him and the woman. He was handsome enough, all right, Flint thought, sizing him up. But there was something about him that didn't ring true.

Right off, he couldn't put his finger on the reason for that feeling. It wasn't because the man was dressed flamboyantly and expensively, though Flint did have a tendency to scoff at such attire. Nor was it because he had a receding hairline that he tried to cover up by combing too much hair to one side. That merely drew a cynical smile from Flint. His attitude. Yeah, that was it. He thought he was better than the average person.

The woman stiffened suddenly and edged backward, but not before a heated argument had ignited. Mere snatches of their conversation reached Flint's ears, but it was obvious they were both upset, especially the woman.

Only after the man raised his voice did Flint realize just how volatile the exchange was.

"I'm warning you," the man hissed.

Although color surged into the woman's cheeks, she didn't back down. Instead, she straightened to her full height, which Flint judged to be about five foot eight, and looked at the man eye-to-eye. But her comeback was lost on Flint as the voice on the intercom chose that moment to announce another flight.

Whatever she said caused the man's sour face to turn even sourer. After glaring at each other for another long moment, the man pivoted on the soles of his highly polished shoes and stamped off.

The woman seemed to wilt, but then she regained her composure and arranged her features to show none of the turmoil that Flint was certain roiled inside her.

And still he continued his perusal. How long had it been since a woman had piqued his interest? he asked himself with contemptuous amusement. He knew the answer. Not since his wife had walked into the hospital, after he'd been stabbed in the gut, and announced she was leaving him.

Muttering another colorful expletive, Flint tried to shift his thoughts to something more pleasant. He didn't want to think about that time in his life, about how he'd nearly lost his mind and had turned to the bottle to forget he'd failed at both his job and his marriage. The scar tissue inside his heart hadn't toughened nearly enough to allow him that luxury. He doubted it ever would.

But neither did he want to dwell on that lovely woman across the way, who had apparently recovered from her verbal skirmish and once again held court.

In many ways she was like the pompous creep who had just left her. The world and everyone in it revolved around her. Why hadn't he picked up on that before? He'd thought he was a master at spotting her type. He'd lived with one just like her. Yeah, on closer observation, she reminded him of his ex-wife, Madge.

He turned away. He would not let her interest him. He didn't need a woman. Not now—when it had been a year and a half since he'd beaten his drinking problem and taken over the dilapidated ranch his uncle left him. The ranch had given him a new lease on life. Satisfaction swelled in his chest, and holding back a grin, he turned to face the woman again.

As if she sensed she was being scrutinized, she looked abruptly in Flint's direction. Furious at being caught, he tried to avoid her gaze. He wasn't quick enough. Their eyes met and clung. For a moment it was as if a hot current had cut through a formidable ice flow. The atmosphere sizzled.

She smiled. He did not. Jerking his head, Flint forced his attention to the loudspeaker announcing his flight.

"'Bout time," he said under his breath as he reached for his bag and hoisted it onto one shoulder.

Once on board, Flint located his seat next to the aisle without any trouble. He buckled up and tried not to think about how much he'd give for a cigarette. That thought magnified when he looked up and saw the dark-haired woman staring down at him.

"Excuse me," she said. "I think that's my seat next to you."

Two

Cursing silently, Flint stood. Of all the passengers who could have been his seating companion, why did it have to be *her?*

While she passed in front of him, he stood rigid, careful their bodies didn't touch. Still, in the process her perfume assaulted his nostrils and her hair grazed his face. He jerked back as if he'd been slapped by a rude hand. But the damage had been done.

"Sorry," she murmured breathlessly before dropping into her seat.

Once seated, she kept her eyes averted. His tension seemed to have communicated itself to her. After fastening her seat belt, she made a big deal of reaching down and fumbling through her travel bag. Flint watched as she pulled out a magazine that had something to do with the jewelry industry and began thumbing through it.

Figures, he thought with a smirk. This lady and fancy baubles seemed to go together. Through narrowed eyes, he continued his guarded perusal of her, his curiosity heightened. A sudden intuition told him this woman represented a danger to him. He scoffed at the idea.

Disgusted with his train of thought and his absurd reaction to this woman, Flint tightened his face and turned his attention to the activities inside the cabin. The flight attendants scurried up and down the aisle checking seat belts and other things pertinent to takeoff. Many passengers were already asleep. Others were reading or chattering with fellow companions.

Flint rubbed his forehead, wishing the flight was over and he was in his truck driving to the ranch. He couldn't wait to start applying the techniques he'd learned in Little Rock. His friend and closest neighbor, Ed Liscomb, would be interested, too, as he was also dabbling with the Brahngus cattle.

More than that, Flint couldn't wait to get off this damned plane and away from this sweet-smelling woman who continued to play havoc with his hormones.

He didn't know how he knew she was looking at him, but he did. Was it because he was so aware of everything about her? Reluctantly he faced her, though he made sure there was no repeat performance of a while ago. He refused direct eye contact.

She was smiling. "I'm Stephanie Marsh."

Classy name for a classy broad, Flint thought churlishly. "Flint Carson," he muttered. Even to himself, his voice sounded rough, like sandpaper. He coughed and turned away, certain she'd get the hint that he didn't want to be disturbed.

She didn't. She leaned closer, as if lessening the distance between them would abate his obvious hostility.

"Do you think the weather will hold?"

"Couldn't say."

Much to his dismay and discomfort, his short answer still didn't give her the hint. She remained where she was, so close the elusive perfume she wore seemed to become embedded in his flesh. He squirmed in his seat.

His long legs weren't made for such close quarters. But he knew it wasn't the seats that caused his discomfort, and that made him that much madder.

"I don't know about you, but I hate the thought of taking off when the sky is overcast, like now," she said, chattering as if he were giving her his undivided attention. "How about yourself?"

Her voice sounded husky. Or was raspy a better word? He cleared his throat, then drawled, "Don't have an opinion one way or the other, ma'am."

"Am I bothering you?" she asked bluntly.

Startled, Flint brought his head up just enough so that again their eyes connected. She had the most enormous direct blue eyes he had ever seen. They crawled up and down him like live things, missing nothing.

"Are you always this outspoken?" he countered equally as bluntly.

Her delicately drawn features betrayed a curious stillness. Only her heavy-lashed eyes alluded to the fact that she was ill at ease.

"Well?"

A tinge of color surged into her face, and she gave a short laugh. "Not usually," she said, looking away, then back, clearly uncomfortable under his direct gaze.

Nothing concrete showed on his boldly carved features, but his dislike of this ongoing conversation was obvious.

With a deep sigh, he finally dragged his gaze away. What was with her, anyway? It didn't take a rocket scientist to figure out he didn't want to talk. Hell, she didn't look dense. So why didn't she just mind her own damned business?

He set his mouth and listened to the flight attendant talk on the intercom.

"Ladies and gentlemen, welcome aboard..."

The voice went on, but Stephanie didn't listen. Her attention was on Flint. Though his face was averted, she continued to watch him, watch the way the muscles in the back of his neck and shoulders rippled, then bunched.

He was tense and uncomfortable. Good, she thought, only to ridicule herself for such childish behavior. But that feeling of remorse was short-lived. Although she had no idea what caused this rude and surly man to feel this way, she took great pleasure in the fact that he did.

Her gaze leveled on him. He was a redneck if she'd ever seen one. He was handsome, though, albeit in a rough-and-tough sort of way. A straight nose, strong jutting chin and rigid mouth added to his aura of remote inaccessibility. He could easily qualify for the Marlboro cigarette billboards, she thought, remembering the way his green eyes had pierced hers from under thick eyebrows that almost met.

As a rule she was not drawn to the rough cowboy type. They were a turnoff. She liked her men more refined, more gentlemanly. Nevertheless, she was attracted to this one.

Why? What was so intriguing about him? Was it because he showed no interest in her? Though Stephanie was totally without conceit, she knew that no matter where she went, she drew attention. Men looked at her.

But a relationship with a man was the last thing she wanted or needed. One broken engagement was enough for her. What she wanted was to make her jewelry business successful and to maintain her hard-won independence from a domineering mother.

Having grown up in a family where money was in abundance, she'd never wanted for anything except that independence. The fact that she was an only child of divorced parents hadn't helped, either, especially as her father was now dead.

Stephanie had finished her education at an exclusive girls' school, then had gone to work for Flora in the family-owned real-estate business, a business that would one day be hers. But there was a catch; she didn't want it.

A great lover of the arts and very artistic herself, she had always wanted to work with precious stones. She'd inherited her talent from her grandmother. Only after she'd turned twenty-eight and broken off her tumultuous engagement to David Weston, handpicked by her mother, did she leave the company and pursue that dream.

That was eight months ago, and now Stephanie was riding an emotional high. She had just completed the sale of her career. Thinking about the necklace, with its old mine-cut diamonds and history that dated back to Napoleonic times, brought chill bumps to her skin.

Stephanie's future had never looked brighter. But if she was to maintain that edge and keep her store solvent in the competitive world of the jewelry business, she could not let up. That commitment left no time for personal luxuries such as pursuing another relationship.

Besides, she hadn't found a man who could make her palms sweat and her heart race. David certainly didn't. She had decided no such animal existed.

Stephanie sobered. The last person she wanted to dwell on was her ex-fiancé or rehash the conversation they'd had prior to her boarding the plane. But her mind was determined to backtrack.

She'd gone to Little Rock to conclude a small piece of business with David's elderly aunt, whom she'd come to know and love. Weeks before, at the old lady's request, she had sold several pieces of jewelry for her and had gotten a handsome price, taking no commission for herself. She'd known Cynthia was short of money because David had the nasty habit of freeloading from her.

She'd only been at the airport a short time when she'd received a shock. Seeing David make his way toward her was the last thing she'd expected, even though he was originally from Little Rock and visited his aunt often. Still, she had been certain he'd followed her there this weekend. He hadn't taken their break-up well and had been harassing her with unexpected visits and random phone calls.

"What are you doing here?" she'd demanded, her face flushed.

David's blond eyebrows had shot up. "Now, is that any way to talk to your fiancé?"

"Ex-fiancé," she snapped, wondering anew how she'd ever let her mother ramrod her into a relationship with this man. Oh, he had everything going for him: blond good looks, polished manners, education, breeding. But when it came to character and substance, he was lacking, or at least Stephanie thought so. He had fooled her for a while, but no longer. The thought of him touching her again made her cringe.

His handsome features didn't change, nor did his smooth voice. "I don't see it that way."

"Well, that's the way it is," Stephanie said flatly. Then lowering her voice, she pressed, "Why are you here?"

"In little Rock, you mean?"

"Don't play games with me!"

"I came to see my aunt, of course."

"Liar."

That softly spoken accusation finally rattled his composure. His blue eyes narrowed in challenge. "I'd watch what I said, if I were you."

"Don't you dare threaten me." Stephanie's eyes flashed fire. "I resent you following me, and I want to know why you did."

David stepped closer. "You know why."

"No, I don't. Suppose you enlighten me."

He was so close now, Stephanie could see the tiny hair positioned in the center of the mole on his right cheek. For a moment she was mesmerized by it. She wondered if he knew it was there. No, she knew he didn't. He wouldn't allow anything to mar his looks. If the situation hadn't been so serious and she hadn't been so mad, she might have laughed.

"You're not going to get away with it, you know."

"Look, David . . ."

"No, you look," he countered. "I want you to return Cynthia's jewelry to her."

"What!"

"You heard me."

"I'll do no such thing."

"Oh, yes, you will. Those weren't hers to sell."

"And just whose were they?"

"Mine."

"Yours?" Her tone was incredulous.

"She promised them to me."

"Well, until she dies, they're hers to do with as she sees fit. And she saw fit to sell them."

"Unsell them."

Stephanie tossed her head. "That's crazy. *You're* crazy. Anyway, the deal I made with your aunt is none of your concern."

"That's where you're wrong."

"Go away, David." Even to her own ears, her voice sounded tired. "Leave me alone and leave your aunt alone. Haven't you put us both through enough grief already?"

His mouth curved in a sneer. "If you don't get that jewelry back, you'll really know what grief is."

"I told you—don't threaten me."

"I'm warning you!" His voice had risen, and he'd lowered it only after he'd realized everyone around him was gawking. "And you damn well better listen."

She'd stared at him coldly, then he had turned his back on her and walked away.

"You haven't heard the last of this," he had hissed to her back.

Now, as Stephanie forced her mind back to the moment at hand, back to the plane's whining engines, she was still miffed that David continued to disrupt her life. Maybe her sorority sister in Austin was right. Maybe she should put some distance between herself and David, at least for a while. The thought of visiting Amy's bed-and-breakfast retreat in the hill country was suddenly appealing. She made a mental note to call her friend when she got home, and firm up her plans.

It galled her, though, that David had any influence over her at all and that she took his threats seriously. Deciding she wasn't going to let thoughts of David further dampen her spirits, she stole a glance at the man next to her. He appeared as uptight as ever and just as mysterious.

A brief smile touched her lips, and at the same time she ignored the nervous flutter in her stomach. Why not? she thought. Why not strike up another conversation? If nothing else, it ought to be interesting.

She tapped him on the shoulder. "By the way, what did you say you do for a living?"

Three

———

"**I** didn't."

Stephanie sighed, but when she spoke, her voice was even. "No, I guess you didn't. And what's more, you don't intend to. Right?"

Something close to a scowl altered his expression. "Are you just curious, Ms. Marsh, or simply bored?"

His brusqueness seemed to have little effect on her. She smiled. "Maybe a little of both, Mr. Carson."

"Well, at least you're honest."

Her smile was disarming. "Maybe too honest for my own good."

He shrugged and turned away. What had he done to deserve this? Again, all he wanted was to be left alone. It was safer that way and much less painful. He'd learned that the hard way as a child. As the memory of those years rose to the forefront of his mind, his lips twisted into a grimace. To this day they haunted him.

He could still hear the kids in his school taunt him, call his names because his jeans were too short and too tight. And the teachers were as bad, but in a different way. Sympathy shone from their eyes when he couldn't produce the latest craze in lunch buckets filled with goodies, much less money to buy a hot lunch.

He had learned that if he kept to himself, he didn't have to endure shame and humiliation. In his solitary world, there were no peers to judge him, no class distinctions.

When he met Madge, years later, things changed. He changed. Before he realized it, she'd ripped that protective covering off him and shown him what he'd been missing. For a while he'd joined the world of the living. But when their marriage started to sour along with his job, he retreated back into himself.

And he'd be damned if he was going to let any woman, no matter how enticing, penetrate that barricade. No sir, he wasn't about to get mixed up with a woman.

"I've found that in my line of work honesty pays off," she said at last, effectively breaking into his thoughts.

He inclined his head in a mock salute. "Is that a fact?"

"If you're not honest, you don't last long in my business."

Flint felt a smile loosen his lips. He'd have to hand it to her, she had guts and determination. Most people would have given up long ago, especially after they'd received one of his cold, bitter stares. But not

Stephanie Marsh. His coldness hadn't deterred her in the least. Yet he sensed her behavior was out of the norm. Gut instinct told him this. There was a nervousness about her that seemed out of place.

"It's the same in my business," he said, admiration neutralizing his tone.

"And just what would that be?" She laughed deep in her throat and angled her head. "I'm not going to let you off the hook, you know."

He permitted his droll humor to surface briefly. "I didn't imagine you would."

"So?"

"So I'm getting started in the cattle business," he added rather reluctantly.

"Oh, so you're a rancher?"

His laugh was sarcastic. "I wouldn't say that."

"I don't understand."

"No, I'm sure you don't." His voice was rough.

"I don't know anything about cattle." She gestured with her hands, then eased an errant strand of hair behind a delicate ear. Never once did she take her blue eyes off him.

"We're even. I'm sure I wouldn't know anything about what you do." His gaze fell to the magazine. "Especially if jewelry's involved."

She threw him a challenging look. "We'll just have to correct that, won't we?"

He steeled himself against the warm femininity she exuded. "I don't think that's..."

"Oh, come on, tell me about your cows."

The way she said *cows* made him smile.

"You ought to do that more often, you know?" Stephanie teased.

She'd caught him off guard. "What?"

"Smile. It does wonders for you."

Unsettled and disturbed, he turned away without answering.

"So, I'm waiting."

The smile no longer in place, he faced her again. "They're a cross between Black Angus and Brahman bulls."

"They sound mean," she said, shivering.

"They are."

She didn't get a chance to respond. Nor did Flint.

The pilot's voice claimed their attention. "Ladies and gentlemen, I apologize for the delay. But we've been cleared for takeoff and should be in the air momentarily. Flight attendants prepare for takeoff."

"Thank goodness," Stephanie muttered. "I'm ready to get this over with."

Flint gave her a curious look. Her face was now minus its color. "You don't like flying?"

"Let's put it this way. I feel better once we're off the ground." A half smile lengthened her lips. "What about you?"

"Same here."

"It seems that every time I get ready to take a trip, planes start to fall out of the sky."

"That's why I try to avoid the news as much as possible," Flint said, and watched her grip the armrest as the engines revved. Shortly, the big plane raced down the runway, then soared upward.

He kept his eyes on her and watched as she visibly relaxed. That was when he realized he'd been almost as uptight as she was, but not because of a fear of flying. Smothering an expletive, he focused his gaze on the front of the cabin.

"So where were we?" she asked.

He didn't pretend to misunderstand. "You were gonna tell me about your work."

"I'm warning you. You may get more than you bargained for."

Although he wasn't looking at her, his faint smile came and went. He couldn't believe it, but he was doing what he swore he wouldn't do. Here he was conversing civilly with a woman, something he hadn't done since Madge divorced him.

"Estate jewelry sales have come into their own of late," she said.

"Is that your business?"

"That's it. Six months ago I opened a small shop in Houston and right now I'm mostly handling antique jewelry." Her voice rose with excitement. "Later, though, I hope to add other related items such as antique dresser silver, sewing kits, which include thimbles and sterling embroidery cases." Stephanie paused. "And then there are your fine laces..."

He shook his head. "You might as well be talking Greek."

Her laugh was a free and warm sound, and for a minute his heart skipped a beat. Promptly he cursed himself for his foolishness.

"Even if I went into it, you'd still be lost. But to simplify it as best I can, I deal in antique jewelry, both costume and colored gemstones."

"I'm still lost."

"All right. See if this makes sense. Garnets, for example, are considered colored gemstones. And though the gemstones interest me the most, I sell a lot of seed pearls and sterling silver.''

In spite of himself, Flint was curious, though he'd have to admit that it wasn't the details of her work that held him, but the woman herself. Every gesture, every smile, every flash of her eyes cut through him. He cleared his throat. "So do you have to wait for people to die to get that kinda stuff?''

His choice of words drew another laugh. "No. Although I do get a lot of it that way.''

"Go on.''

"I haunt flea markets, although there you have to be really careful. Quarterly I set up a booth at the International Show at Market Hall in Dallas. But my main sources are attorneys who settle estates and trips to the English countryside.''

Flint blinked. "English as in England?''

"The same.''

"Must be nice.''

If she detected the sarcasm edging his tone, she didn't show it. "Oh, it is. It's great fun. You never know what you'll find, either.'' Her eyes mirrored the smile on her lips. "Once, in this obscure village, I came across a mother lode of great stuff. I bought a five-piece Victorian parure set for a song.''

"Sounds like something to eat.''

Again she laughed deep in her throat. "Far from it. Actually it's a matched set of earrings, choker, bracelets and rings made up of garnets and seed pearls. These were without exception given to the bride by a groom before the marriage. Only a fast girl would have worn them beforehand.''

"Of course,'' he said drolly.

"As ludicrous as it sounds, it was true."

"So how do you know you're not buying junk?"

"Most of us use a loupe, which is a jeweler's eye-glass. Also, I carry a diamond probe in my purse."

"Sounds lethal."

Again she laughed. Again he shifted in his seat.

"It's a simple little electronic device that's small enough to put in your purse. It tells you if the stone's a diamond or a zircon."

"I'll be damned."

"l'm boring you to death with all this, I know, but once I get started I don't know when to quit." Her laughter tempered to a sheepish smile, and there was a faint blush at the base of her throat. He wondered what it would be like to touch that exact spot with his lips.

"Pray tell who minds the shop while you're doing all this?" He spoke brusquely to distract his thoughts from their unwelcome path.

"A dear friend who hopes to one day become a partner."

"Sounds like you've got it made."

"As a matter of fact I do." Her face shone, which made her all the more beautiful. "Recently I turned a deal that allowed me to set up shop and become truly competitive in a very cutthroat business."

When he didn't respond, she went on in that same lilting voice. "Actually I made two wonderful deals. The first one was a find of a lifetime, at an estate sale. A woman was auctioning off her grandmother's pos-sessions. The necklace I bid on and got came with a history that dated back to Napoleon. But it was only after another jeweler confirmed my appraisal that I knew what I had.

"I went back to the woman and asked her if she'd like it back and she said no, that she was satisfied with the money I'd paid her. You can't imagine how excited I was..."

No, he couldn't, Flint thought, scowling silently, never having had that luxury. She was everything he wasn't. She *had* everything he *didn't*. She had class. He had none. She was high society, and he was a washed-out agent struggling to become a rancher. Resentment kicked up inside him as the string of his past failures paraded one by one through his mind, not to mention the gamble he was taking with the cattle, which had yet to pay off.

"You're not listening to me, are you?"

Through the silence that yawned between them, her voice sounded feeble.

When he didn't answer, she went on. "What's...the matter?" Her voice faltered again. "Did I say something wrong?"

"No," he muttered tersely, unable to meet her puzzled gaze.

Stephanie opened her mouth to speak, only to close it as a flight attendant and beverage cart stopped beside Flint.

"Would you care for something to drink?" Her glance swept both of them.

"Thanks, I'll pass."

"Water for me, please," Stephanie said.

Long after the attendant had moved on, silence prevailed. Stephanie sipped her water and ignored him. She was upset, and he didn't blame her. He'd acted like a jerk, but he sure as hell wasn't going to apologize. It was better this way, anyhow. This trip would soon end, and he would never see her again.

He stole a glance at her and watched as she tipped her head back and took another sip of water. The column of her throat was absurdly vulnerable in the sunlight.

He bit his lower lip to stop a blistering expletive from escaping his lips, just as the plane hit a pocket of air turbulence. The glass bounced off his chest, and water saturated his lap.

"Oh, no!" She raised horrified eyes to his and for a moment neither moved or spoke. Finally Flint's muttered curse forced them into action.

"Oh, God, I'm so sorry," she said, clearly rattled. "Here, let me help." She then grabbed the two napkins off her tray and dabbed at Flint's thighs.

With a sharp intake of breath, he stilled her hand. His fingers felt the fragile bones of her wrist, which were almost exposed through the screen of flesh. Then, as if he'd been stung, he dropped her hand.

Her expression was difficult to read as she lowered her flushed face and once again attacked the stain in his lap.

"Don't," he said in a strangled voice, grappling to get his handkerchief out of his back pocket.

"Please, let me help."

"No, I..." The words died in his throat as her hand accidentally encountered the hardness between his legs. They both froze. Then swearing, he pushed her hand away.

Had she felt the bulge under his fly? Of course she had, you idiot. If nothing else, her sharp, indrawn breath and wide, shocked eyes were dead giveaways.

"Look, stay the hell away from me."

"Flint?"

"Give it a rest. Just give it a rest, okay?"

Stephanie swallowed a biting retort, put her head back and squeezed her eyes shut. But she couldn't stop her face from flaming or her heart from racing. Anger as well as dismay kept it puffing like an out-of-control engine.

How could she have been so careless? But it was an accident, and no matter how well-endowed he was, it didn't excuse his rude behavior. And she wasn't entirely blameless in the charade, either. He'd made it clear from the get-go that he didn't want to be bothered. She'd kept on, though, until she'd forced him into a conversation that soon turned into a confrontation.

When had things started to go wrong? Long before the incident with the water, that was for sure. What had made his face turn back to concrete and his eyes narrow into dark slits? Something she said had obviously turned him off.

The bottom line was she should have curbed her nervous chatter and labeled her fascination for him an indulgent but passing fancy and let it go at that. Only she hadn't.

Well, who cared anyway? She certainly didn't. Mr. Flint Carson wouldn't have to worry about her the remainder of the trip.

Feeling good about her decision, she willed herself to relax, determined to sleep. At that precise moment something went haywire. A loud sound assaulted her ears. An explosion? Was that it? Before she could answer the question, the plane vibrated.

A passenger screamed. Another cursed. Another stood up and yelled for the attendant.

Stephanie bolted upright in her seat and turned toward Flint. She opened her mouth, but only a squeaky sound came out. Fear, like a cold blade of steel, constricted her throat. Her mouth turned dry. Her lips went white. She could feel the hair on her neck bristle and stand on end.

"What...what was that?" she finally managed.

"The engine. Something's happened to the—" He got no further. Without warning, the plane took a violent nosedive.

"Oh, my God," Stephanie cried, "we're going to crash!"

Four

———

Stephanie blinked, then rubbed the back of her hand across her eyes. A ball of pressure swelled inside her chest, a threatening suffocating malaise. *Help! Someone help me!* But why did she need help? The pressure built and thrust its way into her lungs until her cry came out a sob. She forced her eyes open.

At first she couldn't control her vision. But then she saw an outline of a man. He stood beside her. She blinked again, several times trying to bring his face into focus. When she succeeded, she recognized him, yet she didn't.

"Stephanie?"

Stephanie? Who is that? Was he talking to her? If so, she didn't recognize that name.

She shut her eyes again and dug her fingernails into the palms of her hands. Where was she? What was all that noise? Why was she lying down? Questions with no answers swirled through her head. They made her dizzier than ever.

If only she could *think*. But she couldn't. Her mind, in its present state, simply refused to function. Her head pounded as though someone were driving nails through it.

"Stephanie, are you awake? Can you hear me?"

Once more she slowly opened her eyes, and this time everything was focused. The tall, lean man who had been there moments before was still there. A plastic bandage covered one eyebrow, and his features were drawn and pinched.

Stephanie resisted the urge to give in to panic. Instead, she forced herself to speak. "Yes... I can hear you. But who's... who's Stephanie?"

She watched as the lines in his forehead deepened, forcing his eyebrows to point toward the center.

"You're Stephanie," he said. "Stephanie Marsh."

She licked her parched, dried lips and struggled to her elbows.

"Hey, take it easy," he cautioned, helping her until she was in a full-fledged sitting position.

Taking him at his word, she sat still and took deep gulping breaths. The silence that followed trembled with the pounding of feet against the tiled floor. The air was clogged with the smell of medicine, of burning cloth, skin. She felt her stomach turn over.

"Are you all right?" His eyes on her were disturbingly gentle.

She didn't respond. Finally, when the room settled, Stephanie realized she was in a hospital, on a stretcher in what looked to be a hallway. *And I don't know who I am!*

"What . . . what happened?" she whispered at last, looking at him through dazed and disoriented eyes. Then before he could answer, she hurled another question at him, "I know you, don't I?" She clutched at his hand. "Please, tell me I know you."

"Shh, take it easy," he said again. "Yes, you know me. I'm Flint Carson."

"What . . . what happened?" She choked on the words, unable to keep the tremor out of her voice.

Flint eased himself down beside her on the gurney, then disentangled his hand from hers. "Our plane crashed . . ."

Her cry was tremulous.

A spasm of emotion she couldn't identify crossed his face. "You don't remember the crash?"

"Oh my God, oh my God," she whispered. "I can't remember anything." Her voice rose several octaves. "Did . . . did many survive?"

"About half."

Another sob tore loose. "Where . . . did it happen?"

"In a pasture near Crockett."

"And this is the Crockett hospital?"

He nodded. "But it's not equipped to take care of all the injured. That's why you're in the hall."

"Why can't I remember any of this?" she wailed, and pushed a clump of hair behind one ear, only to then wince.

"Watch out," Flint said. "You hit your head."

"I . . . seem to be fine otherwise, though."

"True, except for the bruises on your arms and legs."

"What about yourself?" She wiped the tears from her eyes with the back of her hand, then fastened her eyes on his bandage. "Were you . . . hurt?"

"I'm fine," he said brusquely. "You don't worry about me."

Her lower lip began to tremble, and she looked at him with terrified eyes. "I...I can't believe I...don't know who I am...or where I live!" She grasped Flint's hand again and clung to it.

Before he could respond, a shadow fell over them. Dressed in a white coat, a short, bald-headed man with a tired-looking face stood unobtrusively beside Flint.

Flint calmly withdrew his hand from Stephanie's and stood. "Hello, Abe."

Dr. Abe Powell only had eyes for Stephanie. "Well, it's good to see you awake, young lady."

In spite of her own devastating circumstances, Stephanie's heart went out to him. Like Flint, he looked exhausted. Yet he had the kindest, most sympathetic eyes she had ever seen. "Why can't I remember anything?" she asked in a strident voice, and once again fought off the panic that churned inside her.

Dr. Powell replaced Flint beside her and took both her hands in his. "You let me worry about that. Despite our limited capabilities, we're going to do what's best for all concerned, including you."

Stephanie tried to smile her gratitude, but even that was too much of a chore. She was starting to feel as exhausted as her companions looked. To move one bone or one muscle proved excruciatingly painful.

"I think she's about to fold on us, Abe." Flint's words came out in a rush.

Stephanie raised her eyes to him. "No... I'm not. It's just that I'm... I'm so tired," she said, and watched his expression darken with concern. Or was it anger?

"You're suffering from amnesia more than likely caused by the lick on the head," Dr. Powell said, "but we'll know more when we do the CAT scan."

"How... long will it last—the amnesia, I mean?" Her voice was a mere whisper.

The doctor sighed. "I'm afraid I can't answer that. You could remember everything within the hour. Or it could be days or months or—"

"Not... ever," Stephanie finished for him.

"I doubt that, my dear. But for now we'll take one day at a time."

Stephanie's eyes sought Flint. "Do... do you know anything about me?"

"Only that you own an antique jewelry store in Houston and that you spoke with a man just before you boarded the plane." Before she could ask the questions that quivered on her lips, Flint told her everything he knew about that incident.

"There's nothing else, you're sure?"

"I'm sure." Flint's voice sounded pinched as he and the doctor exchanged looks.

Stephanie massaged her forehead, feeling her hopes fade. She had felt so confused and afraid—trapped in the body of a stranger.

"Why don't you lie back now?" Dr. Powell said. "I'll have a nurse bring you something for your head."

"What's going to happen...to me...?" Wild-eyed, she looked around. Controlled pandemonium, but pandemonium nonetheless, still ruled the day. Doctors and nurses shouted orders. Each vied to be heard over the other.

Candy stripers, office workers and what looked like every other able-bodied person in the town scurried about doing what they could to take care of the injured. And the dead—she wouldn't...couldn't bear to think about them. Not now, anyway.

"We'll take care of you, that's what," Abe said.

"But...I...I shouldn't be taking up space here."

"You let us worry about that." Dr. Powell's calm but slightly gruff voice soothed her so that she could pay attention to what else he said. "Right now, rest is the best tonic for you."

"But...but..."

Flint uncurled his body from against the wall and jumped into the conversation for the first time in a long while. "I second that motion." He jammed his hands into his pockets and transferred his gaze to Stephanie's pale face. His eyes darkened. "You took one helluva lick to the head."

"Flint's right. And while I don't think there's anything to be concerned about, you must be checked."

Stephanie nodded mutely.

"After we get the results of the tests, we'll talk." Dr. Powell stood then and gave her a reassuring nod. "In the meantime, you follow my orders."

"Abe, I'll be along in a minute to help," Flint said.

The doctor paused and brought his stooped shoulders back around. "Everything seems to be under control. Anyway, you've more than done your part."

"Doesn't matter. I'm still needed."

Abe smiled wearily. "Thanks."

Once the doctor had shuffled off, Stephanie's eyes turned to Flint. "You're . . . not leaving, are you?"

"Just to help, that's all."

"What . . . what about afterwards?"

"I suppose I'll rent a car and drive to my ranch."

"Oh, please, you can't!" Stephanie couldn't keep the desperate note out of her voice as she endeavored to stand.

Flint rushed toward her. "For crying out loud, stay put. You're not nearly as strong as you think you are."

His harsh voice had the desired effect. Stephanie fell against the pillow. "You're right," she said shakily, "I'm not."

He didn't respond.

"Will you stay with me during the test?" she asked softly, and watched again as his expression changed.

"I . . ." he began.

Sensing he was about to refuse, she cried, "Please!"

"Damn!" he muttered, clearly at a loss as to how to deal with this sudden turn of events.

Stephanie quivered. "Please?"

She knew she was being selfish and God was probably going to get her because Flint was needed. Though at the moment, he looked as if he needed a bed more than she. Still, she couldn't stand the thought of being separated from him. He was the only sane thing in all this insane mess that had suddenly become her life.

"Please, don't . . . leave me," she whispered.

He swung back around. "All right, you win," he said, sounding drained to the bone. "I won't leave you."

Flint scrutinized Abe's tired face. "You look like you've had it, man. You sure you're gonna make it?"

They had met in what was now the deserted doctors' lounge, which moments before had been occupied by several other weary doctors. They had passed them going out as they were coming in.

"No," Abe said, helping himself to a can of fruit juice in the refrigerator. "But I have no choice. I'll carry on till I drop. You know that."

Flint almost smiled. "Yeah, I know that."

He and Abe Powell had a history, not a long one, but a history nevertheless. After Flint had been released from the hospital in Houston, he'd been sent here to the Crockett hospital, which was forty miles from his ranch, to finish his recuperation. Abe had been his doctor.

The two of them had gotten into a verbal skirmish the first time they'd met because they were so much alike—bullheaded, stubborn and uncommunicative to a fault. In the end, however, Flint developed a grudging respect for the elderly man and trusted him. He knew Abe felt the same about him. Out of that trust had come friendship.

"What about you?" Abe asked, breaking into the silence. "Are *you* all right?" He cleared his throat. "According to the paramedics you wouldn't stop long enough to let them check you."

Flint shrugged. "There wasn't time. Anyway, I wasn't hurt, and others were. I did what I had to do."

Abe shook his head. "When I think of what you went through—"

"I know," Flint said, his voice unsteady. "When that plane took a nosedive, I just knew it was—" He broke off, unable to go on.

"Curtains," Abe said. "And by rights, it should've been, for all of you. Not many people walk away from a crash like that."

"Do you think she'll be all right?"

"Yes. And I think her loss of memory is only temporary, but I can't say for sure."

"I sure as hell hope so."

Abe rubbed his bald head and eyed Flint carefully. "What's she to you, anyway?"

"Nothing," Flint said flatly.

Abe gave him an odd look. "You meant it, then, when you said you didn't know her?"

"Damn straight, I meant it. Never laid eyes on her till she sat next to me on the plane."

"Holy Moses." Abe took a healthy sip of the juice. When he finished, he wiped his mouth. "All I can say is that you'd never know it by the way she's clinging to you."

Flint tightened his lips.

"So you don't know a thing about her except her name?"

"That's about the size of it. And that she lives and works in Houston."

"Along with a million other people."

"Yeah, right."

Abe sighed.

"For a while, though, I thought I'd struck paydirt. Someone handed me a purse, told me they thought it belonged to Stephanie. But later, when I opened it, it wasn't hers.''

''Damn shame,'' Abe said, and once more rubbed his bald head. ''When things settle down a bit, maybe the airline can help her out, shed some light on who she is.''

''Let us pray.''

A silence fell between them while Abe eased down onto the couch and closed his eyes.

''She practically begged me not to leave her.''

Abe's eyes fluttered open. ''Does that mean what I think it does?''

''Yeah.''

''What are you going to do?''

''Stay with her.''

''And later?''

Flint's features were bleak. ''I wish the hell I knew.''

For Stephanie, the following hours passed in somewhat of a blessed blur. She was taken to X-ray for the scan, then back to the hall where she finally fell into a deep sleep. When she awakened, Flint was sitting in a chair next to the stretcher, his head to one side, his eyes closed. In rest, the exhaustion lines on his face had relaxed.

She seized the opportunity to study him, noting the broad expanse of his forehead, the black-lashed, hooded eyes with their arched brows, the narrow straight nose, the wide mouth and the square, almost heavy jaw. And framing it all was the thick unruly hair. It was a face at once arresting and noncommittal. It demanded attention, but it gave nothing away.

As if sensing he was being scrutinized, Flint opened his eyes and straightened.

Their gazes held while the air seemed to crackle around them. As if to challenge the sensation that held them, Flint bolted out of his chair and faced the nearest window. For the first time, Stephanie felt awkward in his presence. The silence didn't help either; it seemed to gnaw at them both, leaving her to bear the brunt of her tormenting thoughts alone.

She felt empty inside, an emptiness she was powerless to fill. If only there was something she could do to trigger her memory. But how did one go about doing such a thing? Somewhere out there her family, her friends, were worried sick about her.

What about a husband? Her heart almost stopped beating. No. Something told her that she wasn't married. Her breathing returned to normal. Besides, she didn't have on a wedding ring.

So if she didn't have a husband, she surely had a job. Of course, she did. Everyone worked, didn't they? Her clothes, though soiled and rumpled, were quality goods, expensive. That could prove her point.

His low, strong voice interrupted her. "You're not helping matters by worrying."

Something inside her snapped, and because he was close, she took her frustrations out on him. "How would you know?" she lashed out.

He raked his fingers through his hair with raw impatience. "I don't, but..." Her quivering chin stopped his harsh words. "Hey, don't. Don't do that. You've done great so far."

She swallowed a sob and tried to smile. "According to whom?"

"Me."

"Oh, Flint, what am I going to do? I have no place to go—"

Abe opened the door to an adjacent room and without preamble said, "Flint, if you'll help her in here, I have the results of the test."

Once Stephanie was seated in the cubbyhole of an office, Abe smiled at her. "Just as I had hoped, there are no signs of damage, no swelling of the tissue around the brain."

"So what are you . . . saying?" Stephanie asked.

Abe's gaze was direct. "Your loss of memory is not the result of the blow to the head."

"Then why . . . ?" A shiver rolled down her spine.

"Let me finish, and I think you'll understand." Abe paused and leaned against the back of a scarred desk. "You're suffering from what is known as psychogenic amnesia, which in laymen's terms is hysterical amnesia."

"And just what the hell is that?" Flint demanded from his position behind Stephanie's chair.

"The loss of memory usually occurs after some stressful episode or traumatic experience."

"Are you saying I can't recall anything because of . . . of fear?" Restless, Stephanie got up and crossed to the window. She stood there, fighting tears and agonizing over her helplessness.

"That's exactly what I'm saying. When one's life is in jeopardy, fear can do tremendous damage. However, with this type of amnesia, it usually disappears as suddenly as it came on, with complete recovery and only a small chance of recurrence. Meanwhile, though, your behavior will be otherwise unremarkable. You'll remember some things and can function normally.''

"But isn't there something I can do... *you* can do to...'' A single, choked sob tore through her throat.

"I'm afraid not, my dear. We play the time game—wait it out." Abe's eyes held sympathy. "But later, if it doesn't return just as I said, then there's hypnosis and other measures we can take."

Weakness forced Stephanie to return to her seat. From there she looked directly at Abe. "And in the meantime?"

Abe rubbed his jaw. "In the meantime, I insist you stay overnight for observation." When she would have protested, he held up his hand. "But because we do need your bed, I see no reason why you have to stay any longer, except that you don't have anyplace to go." His tone was gentle.

Stephanie's face crumpled. "I..."

"Yes, she does."

Her eyes swung from the doctor to Flint. From the concealing shadows of his Stetson, he acknowledged her shocked stare. His eyes, more black than green, bore down on her with an intensity that contrasted with his relaxed attitude.

"What...?"

Ignoring her, Flint faced Abe. "I'll take her with me to the ranch."

Five

The early morning sky was tinted a delicate shade of yellow. Frothy threads of clouds floated through it. The warm air, filled with the scent of growing things, especially flowers, perfumed the typical East Texas day.

Flint, however, was not concerned with the weather or his surroundings. He was concerned about himself, concerned that he'd truly taken leave of his senses.

Stephanie Marsh, sitting rigidly beside him, bore testimony to that.

He had just pulled the rental car onto the highway, and already he was wired so tightly that he felt he could snap the steering wheel in two with little effort.

What had he been thinking when he'd blurted that he'd take her with him? Hell, he had trouble taking care of himself, much less a woman who didn't even know her own name.

The dilapidated state of his ranch suddenly shook him. He wished now he'd taken more pride in its up-keep, especially inside. At least one bedroom was fairly decent. In his mind's eye, though, he pictured the rest of the house, the mess he'd left—papers strewn everywhere, clothes scattered about, rinsed but unwashed dishes in the sink... He grimaced, won-dering what she'd think, only to mentally kick him-self. What did it matter what *she* thought?

It didn't. But he'd opened his mouth and commit-ted himself, and that was what he cared about, what he was going to have to deal with. But how? He cast a sidelong glance at her and felt that same unidentifi-able emotion that had caused him to bring her home.

She had looked lost, alone, vulnerable. But beauti-ful. If anything, the white cast to her face, the weary droop to her full lower lip, the violet circles under her eyes, added to her beauty, made her look ethereal.

Yet that didn't excuse his actions. Nothing could do that. God, what a mess.

Stephanie moved abruptly. Her thin silk blouse re-vealed the fragile bones in her shoulders. And again Flint was aware of the nipples pressing pointedly against the fabric. He averted his gaze.

Had his actions stemmed from lust? No. Of course not. He hadn't wanted a woman in a long time, and he didn't want one now. So why the swell under his fly when he'd stared at her breast? His own shame and mortification almost made him curse aloud.

Flint was a man who lived by his instincts. They had kept him alive on the job when by all rights he should have been dead. But this crazy impulse scared him. He had avoided a lot of traps in his life, but now he had plunged into one with his eyes wide open. One that he would surely regret.

"Flint?"

The soft-spoken use of his name brought him around to face her.

"Yeah."

"Why...why are you doing this? Why did you agree to take me home with you? Granted, I couldn't stand the thought of staying alone at that hospital, but..."

"I wish to God I knew."

She was clearly hurt by his terse response. "You can stop the car right now, and I'll get out."

"And go where?"

Her chin jutted. "I...don't know."

He watched her silently, put out at his rough handling of her, but shaken by the effect she had on him. She hadn't asked to go home with him. That had been his own dim-witted idea, and it wasn't fair to take his anger out on her.

"Look...forget I said that. Sure it'll be awkward, as I'm certainly not set up for guests, but we'll manage."

"What...about clothes?" she asked hesitantly "I need other things, too."

She didn't look at him, and her face was flushed as if she was embarrassed to ask him for anything. He sympathized with her; he'd hate having to depend on someone else for his livelihood. He'd been down that road. And once was enough.

"You aren't up to shopping, are you?"

"No, not really, but I could try."

"No need. I'll take care of it."

"You will?"

Her tone implied she couldn't imagine him taking care of such things. He cast her a mocking glance. "I will."

"I guess I'll have to trust you, won't I?"

"I guess you will, at that," he said sarcastically.

Another silence.

"As soon as we get to your place, I want to contact the airlines."

The urgency behind her words penetrated the fog in his brain. "I've already thought of that. I also think we should call the jewelry stores in Houston, all of them if we have to." He watched her face brighten. "But, only after you rest and your head stops pounding. Right now you don't need the added stress, unless you want to end up back in the hospital."

Her eyebrows peaked into a troubled frown. "No, of course I don't, only—"

"That settles it, then."

"What's your ranch like?" she asked suddenly, sounding desperate again.

"Run-down. But I'm working like hell to fix that."

"Are you having any luck?"

He shrugged. "The new breed of cattle I'm experimenting with will tell the tale."

"I see."

"No, you don't." He bit out the words. "Your life is so far removed from mine that you don't see a damn thing and never will."

She sucked in her breath before throwing him a fulminating glance.

Cursing silently, he said, "Look...I didn't mean that the way it sounded."

"Forget it," she said tersely. "I realize we're both under pressure."

A waiting, uneasy silence came between them.

"Why don't you put your head back and rest," Flint said awkwardly. "You're going to be fine. Just give it time. And stop worrying."

With that he dragged his gaze off her and back onto the road, while asking himself why he didn't take his own advice.

She wished she could stop worrying. But that was impossible. Until she got her memory back, her mind and heart would remain in turmoil.

She had so much to be thankful for, though. How many people lived through plane crashes? She forced herself to concentrate on the beauty around her, something she was certain she had heretofore taken for granted.

She didn't think she'd ever seen anything as beautiful as the blaze of wildflowers. Bluebonnets, crimson clover, Indian paintbrushes, buttercups and black-eyed Susans grew alongside the highway. And lurking among those were the shocking yellow senecio. No artist's brush, no matter how talented, could capture this beauty. For a while it brought her the peace of mind she so badly needed.

That feeling of tranquility disappeared the minute she stole a glance at the man beside her. Cold reality set in once again. Not only did she not know who she was, but she was dependent on this stranger.

For some crazy reason she trusted him. And Dr. Abe Powell trusted him. For now that was good enough for her. What she couldn't figure out was why he had offered to let her stay at his ranch.

He regretted it; that was obvious. He was the type of man who liked his privacy. She had sensed that about him in the hospital room, and she sensed it more now. Even so, she knew he wouldn't go back on his word.

Why did that offer her so little comfort? Was it because he seemed so intense, as if he were charged with too much angry energy and was looking for an outlet?

Like herself, he wore the same clothes he'd had on yesterday. She watched the muscles flex in his arms as he skillfully maneuvered the car. His skin was a warm honey color and sprinkled liberally with fine dark hair. She was intensely aware of him as a man. She shouldn't be, but she was.

She turned and saw Flint watching her from beneath lowered lids. "Are you...married?" she asked, not thinking.

He turned white. "No."

"Have you ever been?" She knew she should leave well enough alone, especially as he looked as if he were about ready to explode. But something she couldn't put her finger on drove her to delve further.

"I don't think that's any of your business."

"No, I guess it's not," she said, hearing the tremor in her voice and hating herself for it.

A sardonic smile thinned his lips. "I was married once."

"Divorce?"

"Yes."

"I'm sorry."

"Why? I'm not."

An awkward silence ensued.

"Do... do you think I'm married?"

The car swerved slightly. "What makes you think that?" he asked, when the vehicle was once more in control.

"Maybe that man in the airport was my husband."

"No way." The reply came in a strained growl.

"You say that with such conviction."

He shrugged. "Instinct tells me I'm right."

"Is that all?"

"Let's just say I give you more credit."

She puzzled over that, then said, "It sounds like something was wrong with him."

"There was. He's a first-class jerk. And he's not your husband. Just trust me on that."

A short, but seemingly final silence fell between them.

"How much farther?" she asked dejectedly, realizing he wasn't going to say anything else. But then, she knew there was nothing else to say. He'd already told her everything he knew.

"A few yards up the road is the turn to my place," he said.

Feeling her insides constrict, Stephanie closed her eyes. When she opened them, Flint was braking in front of a white frame house that looked badly in need of repair. Her heart gave a decided lurch at the same time she shifted her gaze to Flint.

Reading her reaction, his features turned cold and unbending. "You wished you'd stayed in the hospital, don't you?"

She forced herself to look into that dark face. "No...I—"

"Ah, save it," he said savagely, and opened the door.

She took several deep breaths. They didn't help. Nothing would help except the return of her memory. She couldn't bear to think about the consequences if that didn't happen.

Six

"Well?"

"Well, what?"

Ed Liscomb snorted. "Ah, hell, boy, don't give me that song and dance."

The corners of Flint's eyes crinkled. Ed was the only person he knew who could call him boy and get away with it.

"I'm not going to let you off the hook this time, either," Mary, his wife, put in softly.

Flint rested his mellowed gaze on her. "You mean you're going to side with this old codger?"

Mary smiled, but her eyes were serious. "In this instance yes. When you phoned and told me you had a guest, a woman you didn't even know, I was too stunned to ask questions, but not now."

Besides Lee Holt, his ex-partner at the agency, Ed and Mary Liscomb were the only friends Flint claimed. Generally he didn't like people poking in his business.

But with Ed and Mary, the rules didn't apply. He tolerated their meddling because they were fine people and genuinely cared about him, as much as he'd let anyone care, that is. Two days after he'd taken over the ranch, they had come over and welcomed him. Their spread of several hundred acres lay two miles south of his.

While he was struggling to get started, Ed had it made. Flint suspected his neighbor was actually a millionaire. He'd become successful in oil before the market collapsed. Damned shame they didn't have any children to carry on, their only son having lost his life in a car accident. You would never know they were wealthy, though. There was not a pretentious bone in either of them.

Ed was as tall as Mary was short. Both, however were slender, except for Ed's pot belly. At sixty, his gray beard was full. And his whiskey-toned, boisterous voice evinced his love for beer. Mary, on the other hand, was soft-spoken and attractive with a clear complexion and short hair flecked with gray.

They were kind and generous to a fault. Whether Flint liked it or not, they had taken him under their wing. Mary kept harping, "We're going to humanize you, force you to join the land of the living."

Flint doubted that. He liked his life the way it was and saw no reason to change it. The sooner he rid himself of his guest, the sooner he could get on with it. First, however, he had to explain who his guest was and why she was here.

But simply thinking about Stephanie and her reaction when they had arrived earlier caused his heart to hammer violently. In spite of his vow not to give a damn about what she thought about his place, he found that he did. The living room had looked like a pigsty—worse than he'd remembered. But Stephanie hadn't seemed to notice, or if she had she didn't comment. Fatigue was written on her face, and the top priority had been getting her to the spare bedroom so that she could lie down.

He'd stood awkwardly just inside the door and stared at her. "Er...is there anything you need? How 'bout a cup of coffee?"

A semblance of a smile relaxed her lips, but he noticed she wouldn't look at him. She sensed the strain in the air as much as he did. "No, I'm fine. I just want to rest for a while." He shifted from one foot to the other. "Sure, but if you need anything..."

"Thank you," she had whispered.

That had been several hours ago, and she was still sleeping. Meanwhile he'd called Ed and Mary to let them know he was all right and to ask Mary to purchase a couple of changes of clothes for Stephanie, as well as other items pertinent to a woman's needs. He'd planned to buy the things, but he hated to leave her. She looked so frail, as if a brisk wind could blow her away.

Ed finally broke the lengthy silence. "By the way," he said gruffly, "we're glad you're all right."

"God, yes," Mary added softly. "When we heard about the crash and realized it was your plane...well,

I don't have to tell you what went through our minds."
She broke off with a shudder.

Flint's eyes were bleak. "I sure as hell thought we
were goners."

Ed took a seat beside his wife on the couch and
crossed his arms over his belly. He stared at Flint, who
leaned against the mantel, his features grim. "Well, all
I can say is it wasn't time for your number to be
punched."

"I don't ever want to live through it again," Flint
said roughly.

"What really happened?" Mary asked. "The news
said it was birds, but I find that hard to believe."

"Well, believe it," Flint said tightly. "When the
plane hit them, the fan cut loose from the right engine and ripped a hole in the wing." He snapped his
fingers. "After that, it was quick and devastating."

"Damn!" Ed's voice boomed. "No wonder the
thing went down. It's a miracle anyone survived."

"Only those of us in the front did." Flint's eyes were
suddenly as hollow as his voice.

Mary's eyes were wet. "So... so it was those poor
souls in the rear who... who died."

"Most of 'em, yes," Flint said.

"How you were able to function enough to help is
beyond me," Mary put in. "I'd have been so shaken
up, I would've been paralyzed."

"No, you wouldn't, hon," Ed said, facing his wife.
"You'd have rolled up your sleeves and pitched right
in, just as Flint did, and helped as many people as you
could."

Mary wiped a tear off her cheek. "Maybe...I don't
know."

"Well, it was a few hours out of hell, I can assure you," Flint said. He took his Stetson off and tossed it onto the back of the nearest chair. "I worked on pure adrenaline, but I've never felt so useless or frustrated." He paused. "Or seen so much suffering."

Again Mary shuddered, and the room fell silent. "So is that why you brought this woman here?" she asked at last.

Ed stood and joined Flint at the fireplace, propping a booted foot on the hearth alongside Flint's. "Yeah, back to your...er...house guest. It's obvious she wasn't seriously hurt..."

Flint released a pent-up sigh, then answered reluctantly, "No, not too bad."

"So why is she here?" Mary was clearly baffled, and it showed in both her face and her voice.

"She took a lick on the head," Flint said, his gaze including them both, "which caused temporary amnesia."

"Oh, no," Mary said with a frown. "That poor woman."

"That still doesn't tell why she's here." Ed's tone was brisk and not nearly as understanding.

"She was sitting next to me on the plane, and I guess she saw me as her savior." Flint's attempt at humor failed. His smile came out a smirk. "Hell, how should I know? It just happened, that's all."

Ed and Mary looked at each other and then back at Flint. They seemed dumbfounded by his actions. But after seeing the dark, closed expression on Flint's face, they realized it was no use questioning him further. He'd said all he was going to say.

"Well, if I . . . we can be of any help," Mary said, "don't hesitate to ask."

"You've already helped," Flint said. "By the way, I need to pay you for the clothes."

Mary stood. "Don't worry about that now."

"I insist," Flint countered, pulling his billfold out of his back pocket and handing Mary several bills. "Does that cover it?" Mary nodded. "Thanks again."

Ed cleared his throat, and when he spoke, his voice was uncharacteristically subdued. "Well, boy, we'd best go now and let you get on with your business. But if you need us, just holler."

"Will do," Flint said.

"Let's get together as soon as you can. I wanna hear about your trip and what you found out."

"I'll get with you in a day or so," Flint said, following them to the door. "Thanks again for everything."

He had just closed the door when he heard the noise. At first he didn't know what it was. But then he heard it again. This time he knew. *Stephanie!*

"Now what?" he muttered, hearing her cry again as if in pain.

With his heart in his throat, he bounded down the hall. The instant he crossed the threshold, he pulled up short.

The moonlight, streaming through the window, allowed him to see every detail of her as she sat in the middle of the bed. Her face, ravaged with tears, looked starkly white under the cloud of dark hair. But it was her body silhouetted underneath the shirt he'd given her to sleep in that drew his attention and held it.

Her shoulders were bare, and he pictured what it would be like to hold her and swallow her up. He gripped the knob, momentarily robbed of his breath. Her beauty took it away.

"Stephanie?" he finally croaked, unable to move. "What's the matter?"

"Oh, please, help me," she cried, turning glazed, feverish eyes on him. But he knew she wasn't actually seeing him. She was in the throes of a nightmare.

"Help me—I'm on fire," she whispered, her shoulders quivering.

He quickly strode to the bed and paused at the edge, near enough to touch her, to smell her. The scent filled his nostrils with a renewed awareness that shocked him. That awareness knocked his relationship to her completely off center. Alarm rose in him.

"Please," she cried, holding her arms up to him.

Blocking out his thoughts, he sat down and pulled her toward him. She latched on to him and placed her fragile body against the rock-hard solidity of his.

"Shh," he began awkwardly, "everything's going to be all right."

Only it wasn't, not for him. Sweat collected, then ran down his body like rain. He shouldn't be holding her like this. With superhuman effort he tried to disentangle himself.

"No," she pleaded, and looked up at him. "Don't leave me."

He didn't want to. Oh, God, he didn't want to. She felt so good, so right. But it wasn't right. It was wrong, wrong, wrong! Cursing silently, he tried once again to put distance between them.

She clung that much tighter and pressed her breasts deeper into his chest.

"No," he said thickly. Even through his shirt, her nipples felt like points of fire. He ached to lick them with his tongue.... His body turned hot with shame. Only his iron will curbed that impulse.

A coldness feathered down his neck, while another wave of heat washed over him so intense it stopped his breath in his throat. He tightened his jaws until the muscles clenched into white ridges, while he placed both hands on either side of her shoulders and gently, but firmly, pushed her back against the pillow.

Mercifully, she had fallen back to sleep.

He didn't get up. He couldn't. He'd have to wait out the damage done to his own body. Hot blood had rushed to his groin when she'd pressed against him. He could scarcely move or breathe.

Flint didn't know how long he remained there before he dragged himself to his feet. He trudged to the door where he turned and watched the steady rise and fall of her chest.

In his own room, a few minutes later, he eyed the bed as if it were something menacing. He might as well not even bother, he thought with a curse.

It was going to be a long night, a very long night indeed.

The sun poked through the flimsy curtains and directly into Stephanie's face. What had awakened her?

She shifted positions, only to flinch. Why was she so stiff? So sore?

Gingerly she opened her eyes and without moving, stared at her surroundings. They meant nothing to her. The room had all the personality and warmth of a hospital room, she thought, and felt an unknown fear rise inside her.

Along with the wrought-iron bed, there was a scarred chest of drawers, and a lattice-back rocker. *Sad neglect* was the phrase that came to mind. *Where am I?*

Like a punch to the stomach, the answer hit her. "Oh, no," she cried. To stifle another cry, she jerked the pillow from under her head and covered her face with it. She was in a strange place with a strange man, and she couldn't remember who she was.

The truth, in that dark moment, was so overwhelming that she thought she'd black out from sheer hysteria. She drew several deep breaths, and the world righted itself once again.

She tossed back the sheet and eased upright, then swung her legs over the side of the bed. She wasn't about to let stiff limbs stop her from getting up. She sat still for a minute and no longer felt dizzy. Her focus was clear as ever. And she was hungry, ravenously so. Had it been the smell of bacon that awakened her? While it smelled too good to pass up, she hesitated a bit longer.

The thought of facing the surly, grim-faced man who was her reluctant host was not pleasant. On the heels of that thought came the unsettling dream she'd had last night. She had dreamt he'd folded her close against him—and remembered how protected she'd felt.

Stephanie's fingers dug into the pillow. Why was her mind playing such mean tricks on her? This man meant nothing to her, except as a means to an end. Was she losing her mind after all? No. She was merely suffering repercussions from the accident.

She had to believe she had done the right thing in coming here. She also had to believe that he'd help her find her identity. Flint was her only hope, as no one else at the hospital had time to worry about her.

She was on her feet when she saw the stack of folded clothes at the foot of the bed. She wondered where they had come from and who had put them there. *He* had been to her room. Her cheeks flamed. She felt her heart beating. Surely he hadn't touched her when he'd brought these things...? No. It had been a crazy dream, and it had meant nothing. When she walked to get the clothes, she noticed her legs had the consistency of jelly.

Later, dressed in jeans, pink shirt and tennis shoes, Stephanie made her way into the kitchen.

He stood in front of the stove. Like her, he was dressed in jeans and a shirt. But where her outfit was new, his was anything but. The jeans were faded and tight fitting, calling attention to his slim hips and powerful thighs. His shirt was worn, too, and hung open, revealing a flat stomach.

Unwittingly, her eyes roamed freely over taut skin bronzed by the sun. She tried to turn away; she tried to ignore that disturbing feeling that curled inside her. She could do neither.

As if he sensed her presence, he looked up. Their gazes connected and held.

Wetting her lips, she stammered, "I...uh...good morning."

Seven

"What are you doing up this early?"

Flint's chilled, coarse voice, so unexpected, stopped her cold. A long moment passed before she could answer him.

"Actually, it's not *that* early. But even if it were, I couldn't stand the bed any longer." She strove to keep her voice casual, refusing to let his boorish attitude get to her. Dismayed, she realized she hadn't pulled it off; she sounded both breathless and defenseless.

He tried to smile, but he didn't pull that off either. The endeavor was merely a meaningless flexing of his facial muscles. "You may as well have a seat. Your breakfast is ready."

She hesitated, her eyes scanning the kitchen. Like the living room, through which she'd just passed, this one was equally cluttered. And dingy. The walls needed painting, as did the cabinets. But first, everything could use a good scrubbing—the curtains, the countertops and the floor.

Apparently she hesitated too long or he again read the censure in her eyes, for when he spoke his voice was insultingly cold.

"I hope you weren't expecting the Hilton, Ms. Marsh."

"Look...I'm—"

He cut her off. "It's too bad we *all* can't have the best of everything."

"I hardly think soap and water would fit into that category."

He raked her with unkind eyes. "I don't give a damn what you think."

"I know you don't, only—"

"And you wanna know something else? Not everyone's born with a silver spoon in their mouths."

Stephanie bristled. "And you think I was?"

"For starters, you don't dress in designer clothes nor do you own a jewelry store unless you have money."

"That's not true," she said hotly. "But in any event, I can't defend myself."

He said nothing for a while, during which Stephanie nursed a frantic need to lighten the mood, but nothing lighthearted came to mind.

Then out of the blue he mumbled, "If I'd known I was going to have company, I would've done some cleaning."

She saw the muscles along his jaw round in knots, and she knew what that must have cost him to say. "I don't want you to think I was criticizing because I wasn't.'' She took a breath and forced herself to go on. ''I'm . . . just grateful for your help.''

''You have a strange way of showing it.''

She didn't want to aggravate an already taut situation so she swallowed another stinging retort and turned away.

After a moment he said, ''So how 'bout some breakfast?''

''Thanks,'' she said, still a bit shaky, but glad he had decided to drop the matter. ''Only don't go to any trouble for me.''

A brief smile lent a fleeting warmth to his features. ''No trouble. You're bound to be hungry.''

''Actually I am.''

''Want a cup of coffee?''

''Sounds good, or at least I think it does.''

He filled a cup of the steaming liquid without responding.

''Thanks,'' she murmured. Instead of sitting down, she crossed to the window behind the table and looked outside. The day shaped up to be a fine one. In a distant pasture, a clump of blue wildflowers swayed in the spring breeze. A huge live oak watched over them while two feisty squirrels used it as a racetrack. Somehow, she knew she'd never noticed something so trivial as nature's pets playing chase. But her brush with death had changed all that. It had changed *her*.

''Okay, so how do you like your eggs?''

Flint's question jolted her. How *did* she like her eggs? ''I . . . I don't know,'' she whispered, swinging around and staring at him.

''Hey, calm down,'' he cautioned as he took in her eyes—twin mirrors of misery. ''It's no big deal. I'll fry you a couple over easy to go along with the bacon and biscuits.''

Stephanie shook her head, having recovered from the shocking reality that something so simple as what she ate for breakfast could turn out to be something so important. ''I have a feeling that's way too much food.''

''I wouldn't think you'd have to worry about your weight.''

His glance appraised her, seeming to linger a moment longer than necessary on her neck, then her breasts, which were unconfined beneath her T-shirt. The bra nestled among the panties had been too small. By the time his gaze reached her eyes again, she trembled inside.

''Every woman has to worry about her weight,'' she said, speaking impatiently to mask her alarm.

But she need not have worried. He no longer looked at her. He concentrated on the task of removing the bacon from the iron skillet and placing it on paper towels to drain. She watched his hands and wondered again if she'd actually felt them on her skin last night or if it had truly been a dream.

Feeling her face suffuse with color, she averted her gaze, appalled at her thoughts. More than that, she was appalled at her behavior. You would think she'd never found a man attractive. Surely that wasn't the case; nor was it the point. Her only concern should be regaining her memory. So why was she focused on this man who begrudgingly offered his hospitality?

''Eat up,'' Flint said.

His abrupt voice and the sound of the plate clattering against the Formica-topped table roused her into action. She moved back to the table and sat down.

They ate in silence, or rather Flint ate in silence. Stephanie took no more than two or three bites of each item, then she pushed her plate away.

He looked up, his eyebrows raised. "Something wrong?"

"No, actually it was delicious."

A smirk crossed his lips. "Yeah."

"It was, really," she said with a fixed smile. "It's just that right now I have a bit more on my mind than food."

Flint shoved his own plate aside and reached for his coffee cup. After taking a sip, he looked at her over the rim. "Nothing yet, huh?"

"Nothing." Her tone was deflated. "Isn't that obvious when I can't even remember whether I like eggs or not?"

"It won't do any good to beat up on yourself, you know."

"I know, but I can't help it. I feel so useless, so frustrated."

"I'll help you any way I can. I told you that, and I meant it. So if there's anything you remember, anything at all..."

"Not so much as a glimmer," she said in a stricken voice. "And that's what scares me, that and the fact that somewhere out there my family is most likely crazy with worry. And..." She broke off and sighed.

"And what," he pressed.

"And I don't have any money..."

"So, I can lend you some."

"I couldn't let you do that."

"Why?"

"I just couldn't."

"Suit yourself."

She squared her thin shoulders. "Besides the money, there's the clothes you . . . chose."

"I didn't choose them."

"Oh." He probably had one of his women friends do the honor, she thought snidely. But she didn't dare ask.

"So what's wrong?" he demanded curtly.

The question caught her off guard. "With . . . what?"

"The clothes," he said impatiently.

"Nothing's wrong with them . . . only . . . all of them don't fit."

"I see." Once again his eyes dipped to her breasts as if he knew exactly which item she was referring to. And once again her face tinged with color, though she tried as before to control it.

"I . . . I don't want you to think I'm ungrateful because . . . I'm not. And as soon as I can, I'll pay you back." Her voice was so husky it was barely discernible.

His eyes moved from the top of her head, over her face and throat, back to her breasts. "Whatever you say."

And quite suddenly they had nothing to say to each other. They realized that simultaneously, and that made the situation more awkward. Their glances met, then fell away as both pretended to examine the room as if searching for something. It was a most unwieldy moment for Stephanie, and in a rash attempt to shift it back into balance, she stood up and once again crossed to the window.

Casually she said, "While I'm here, I . . . I want to earn my keep."

He seemed taken aback by her words, and his lips tightened. "What did you have in mind?"

"That's just it, I don't know."

"The doctor's orders were for rest."

"I will, but I can't just . . . freeload."

"It's okay by me." His tone was mocking.

"I could clean your house."

He shot out of his chair, and in a split second he loomed over her. "Forget that."

"Are you going to snap my head off every time I say something you don't like?"

He backed away. "Hadn't planned on it."

"So, let me help," she pressed with a forced smile, determined not to let him further intimidate her, suspecting his bark was much worse than his bite. "I'm sure if I dabbled in antique jewelry, I'm bound to like antique houses."

His dry laugh sounded like cornstalks rubbing together. "Think so, huh?"

"Sure. Besides, this place has possibilities." She was warming to the subject, or was it his sudden good humor?

He held up his hand. "Whoa. I might let you tidy up a bit, but nothing else. And only after you're stronger."

That hard note was back in his voice, but she ignored it. "Have you ever thought of improving it?"

"Yeah, a million times, only I don't have the money."

That stopped her cold, and she didn't know what to say, so she didn't say anything. Finally, to relieve the heavy silence, she asked, "Have you always been a rancher?"

"No."

Deciding that getting the desired information out of him would be like pulling eye teeth, she went about it with a tenacity disguised by her casual manner. "So how did you make your living?"

"I worked for the DEA."

She didn't try to mask her shock. "But...that's the Drug Enforcement Agency."

"One and the same."

"And you don't work for them anymore?" she pressed.

"Technically, I'm on a leave."

"Did something happen?" She knew his patience was running out. In fact, she'd expected him to tell her to go to hell long before now.

"Yeah, you might say something happened. A drug bust went sour, and I got carved up like a piece of meat."

Stephanie's face lost its color.

"Satisfied?" he demanded harshly.

"I'm...I'm sorry. I didn't mean to..."

He reached for a battered Stetson and jammed it on his head. "Forget it. I have."

She stood, and with her heart pumping as though she'd just run a marathon, she started toward the door.

"Where are you going?"

She stopped. "To...my room."

"Good, be ready, say, in about fifteen minutes."

"For what?" she asked, startled.

"We're going into town so you can keep your appointment with Abe." He paused. "Afterward, we'll stop by the store so you can...er...exchange that item that was too small."

Heat surged into her cheeks, and she shifted her gaze.

"Well, what are you waiting for?"

She rushed the rest of the way to the door, only to stop and spin around. "Will you tell me the truth?"

"About what?"

She passed her tongue across her dry lips. "Last night."

"What do you want to know?"

"Did you come to my room?"

"You don't remember?"

"No."

"You had a nightmare."

She peered down at the floor then back up. "So you...you did hold me?"

"Yes, I held you." He opened and closed his mouth, as if strangling.

A second lapsed into a minute, and still neither spoke or moved.

"Thank...you," Stephanie whispered at last.

He allowed his droll humor to surface. "You're welcome."

Another few seconds dragged by.

Finally, Flint said. "Well?"

"Well what?" She took a long, slow breath to steady herself.

"Are you going to stand there all day?"

"No, no, of course not," she said, and turning, fled the room.

She couldn't be sure, but later when she thought about that incident again, Stephanie was certain his laughter had followed her.

Eight

The April wind was blustery. It stood his longish hair on end and hissed through the grass like a reptile. The sun, equally as strong, glared down on him like a petulant god.

Flint ignored both as he took his frustration out on the fence he was fixing. He didn't remember ever hammering a nail so hard into a piece of wood as he was now. He paused and wiped the sweat out of his eyes and off his forehead, but it did no good. The minute he slammed in another nail, sweat drenched him again. Still, he kept working.

Three days had passed since he'd taken Stephanie to town. First, she'd shopped. Then he'd driven her to the doctor's office and sat in on the visit.

In Abe's office, he could still see Stephanie's stricken face, hear her pleading with Abe to help her.

He'd watched from his position against the wall, his arms crossed over his chest.

Stephanie had sat in front of Abe's desk, her eyes large and troubled. "I was sure by now I'd remember something."

"What I told you in the hospital still applies," Abe said patiently. "You can't rush this. So try not to worry—that merely aggravates things. Just continue to take those pills when your head pounds. And don't do anything strenuous."

Now, as Flint hammered another piece of wire onto the fence post, Abe's last warning brought to mind Stephanie's offer to clean his house. Damn! Was that a hoot, or what? Somehow he doubted she'd ever pushed a broom in her life, much less picked up a dust cloth.

Anyway, that was the last thing Stephanie needed to do, especially when she looked so fragile that a light puff of wind could blow her away. But that didn't stop her from looking sexy as hell.

She'd climbed into the truck, and that action had outlined her breasts, instantly defined their roundness—something he didn't want to acknowledge. Yet as much as he ached to deny it, electricity hummed between them and had from the first time they had met.

He'd made it a point to keep his eyes off her and on the road, but that hadn't kept him from shifting uncomfortably behind the wheel. And he still shifted uncomfortably as he reached for another nail.

It was hell to be poor, he thought, driving another nail in. By now he figured he should've been able to hire a full-time hand, but his herd hadn't progressed enough to allow him that luxury.

The only thing worse than being broke was his obsession with Stephanie Marsh. He'd tried to avoid her, had assured himself he'd acquired an immunity against her type. Only he hadn't. She was just too damned attractive.

The feel of her in his arms had reawakened an appetite that he thought had long been buried. She'd been under his roof only three days, and already he had thoughts of her writhing under him, whimpering in climax.

So why didn't he just take her? What could be wrong with feeling again? Maybe in losing himself in her, he might find himself again.

But that wasn't the answer, and he knew it. Even if she let him touch her—which was a big if—making love to her wouldn't work. Their relationship was a dead-end street. He saw no reason to start something that would go nowhere.

His only option was to find out who the hell she was, then send her packing. Flint stared at his jerking hands. He needed a drink in the worst way.

"Stop it, Carson!" he muttered, and sucked air deep into his lungs. He should take the initiative, he knew, hire someone to find out Stephanie's identity. Because of his years in law enforcement, he had connections and was not above using them. All he had to do was pick up the phone to a private-eye buddy in Lufkin.

Yet he hesitated. Why? Could it be he was reluctant for her to regain her memory because she would no longer be dependent on him? Hell! He hoped not. Surely he wouldn't stoop that low?

No, that wasn't the case. He wanted her to leave before he did something stupid, something he'd regret for the rest of his life.

His mind, his thoughts were suddenly in a jumble he couldn't untangle. So rather than try, he packed his things and mounted his horse and headed toward the house.

If it weren't for the loss of memory, she would be pleased with her recovery. Rest had made the difference. She could move now without wincing, and the terrible headaches were at least bearable. Still, she knew she had a ways to go before she could be pronounced one hundred percent fit again.

She was fortunate to be able to relax during the day while Flint worked. At night she was almost afraid to close her eyes. She feared another nightmare would attack her subconscious. She did not want a repeat performance of that first night.

Just thinking about that incident made her uneasy. But then thinking about *him* made her uneasy. In spite of the hospitality, she knew she had severely disrupted his life. Flint resented it, resented her, even though most of the time she couldn't decipher what lay behind those deep green eyes when she'd catch him looking at her.

Despite that, or maybe because of that, he intrigued her and made her want to know what made this lonely man tick.

Stephanie scoffed, however, at such nonsense, reminding herself that she was only a temporary houseguest and nothing more. Besides, she didn't want to mar this beautiful day with dark thoughts.

She finished dressing and walked out of her room, only to come to a sudden halt. She thought at first her eyes were playing tricks on her, but after she blinked she knew better. The living room, while not sparkling, was clean and straight. Flint had been busy.

A smile tugged at her lips. "Well, I'll be damned," she whispered, then wandered into the kitchen. He'd been at work there, too.

With that smile locked in place, she dashed out the kitchen door into the wind and sunlight. The instant she rounded the corner of the house, she saw him. He rode across the pasture, and again she was dumbstruck, held by the sight.

God, but he looked tall in the saddle, man and beast moving as one.

He must have seen her leaning against the fence rail in the backyard, because he immediately reined the horse in her direction.

Her heart raced, and her emotions felt scattered. She tried not to stare, permitting herself only furtive glances, but as he neared, she scrutinized him from his hat down to his scuffed boots. He was a magnificent animal, more perfect than the gelding he rode.

Stephanie tried to kill her thoughts and shift her gaze, but she couldn't, especially after Flint stopped the horse directly in front of her. He sweated profusely, she saw. His hair edging his Stetson was wet, and his shirt was plastered to his sculptured body. He breathed heavily.

She felt herself responding to the pull of that raw magnetism, so strong that it left her weak. And more lost than ever. She didn't even know who she was; she was fighting for her own identity. So how could she think about this man in sexual terms? But he was sexy—mouth-wateringly sexy.

He sat atop the horse and regarded her in silence. His eyes saw through her blouse and burned into the deepest recesses of her body, telling her as plainly as spoken words that he was aware of her thoughts.

Flint then swung out of the saddle gracefully and stood within touching distance of her.

"Hi," she said inanely, her cheeks scarlet.

His smile mocked her. "Hi, yourself."

Silence.

"Er... are you through working for the day?"

"Yeah," he drawled, "I thought I'd knock off and go see Ed."

"Oh." She tried not to show her disappointment at being left alone for the remainder of this beautiful day.

"Wanna come?"

Stephanie liked Mary Liscomb on sight, as well as her bear of a husband. Because of Flint, they welcomed her without pretense.

Anxious to show off their home, Ed and Mary took her on a tour of the gardens before going inside.

The interior was more lush than the outside, Stephanie thought. The floors in the great room and hall were oak and shone like glass. Marble covered the stairs and the entryway. Everywhere the walls were white and the scent of peach potpourri was prevalent.

Ed and Mary insisted they remain for lunch. Even though she felt Flint didn't want to, he gave in to Mary's cajoling.

Now, following a delicious meal, she and Mary were enjoying a second cup of coffee in the breakfast nook off the kitchen while the men discussed business in another room.

"I'll have to admit we were shocked and still are that he brought you home with him." Mary smiled.

Stephanie smiled back at her hostess. "That's understandable."

"Flint just doesn't do things like that," Mary added. "In fact, I've never known him to fly by the seat of his pants, if you know what I mean."

Stephanie smiled again. "I know what you mean. But when I look back, I'm not sure he had much choice." Stephanie admitted.

Mary raised delicate eyebrows. "Oh?"

"You mean Flint didn't tell you that I practically begged him not to leave me?" Even as she confessed this, she felt awkward.

Mary laughed deep in her throat. "Why, honey, talk is the one thing that he doesn't do."

"You're certainly right about that."

"You don't know the half of it. He won't let you do one thing for him unless he can return the favor, which goes to prove that underneath that tough hide is a kind man. You know he's a pilot, don't you?"

Stephanie shook her head, trying to follow Mary's change of thought. "No...no, I didn't."

"That doesn't matter, really. The point I was about to make is that Ed's offered him his plane a number of times, but do you think he's taken him up on the offer? Of course not. He's proud and mule-headed to a fault."

"But you wouldn't change a thing about him, would you?" Stephanie smiled, but her tone was serious.

Mary grinned sheepishly. "We love him like a second son."

"So that must mean you know him well."

"No one knows Flint. He refuses to share himself. I feel that's because he's known more than his share of pain."

"I know he was married." Stephanie was aware she was going on another fishing expedition and felt bad, especially as Mary's reluctance was obvious.

"Yes, but it didn't last." Mary's tone was troubled. "While he was in the hospital with a hole in his side, his wife slapped him with divorce papers."

Stephanie's heart gave an unexpected twist. "How awful."

"That's what we thought. Though, of course, he won't talk about it. So we don't ask or push."

"I just hope I can repay him someday for helping me."

"Oh, honey," Mary said, switching subjects again, "it must be terrible not knowing anything about yourself."

Stephanie took a sip of coffee as if it could stave off the threat of tears. She'd been doing so well keeping her feelings in check. "I feel like I've been tossed in the middle of an ocean without a life jacket."

"That must be awful." Mary reached over and squeezed her hand. "It's a miracle both you and Flint are alive."

"When I get to feeling sorry for myself, I remind myself of that."

"So what are your plans?"

Stephanie thrust a hand through her thick mane. "I don't know."

"So you plan to stay with Flint indefinitely, then?" Mary pressed in a soft voice.

"No . . . no, of course I don't."

Mary watched her carefully. "You're welcome to come and stay here, if you'd like. It's just Ed and me milling around in this big house by ourselves."

Stephanie should have expected the invitation, but she hadn't. And though she was touched by Mary's offer, the thought of leaving Flint filled her with panic. Crazy as that sounded, it was the truth. But she couldn't tell Mary that. "I . . ."

"You think about it," Mary cut in quietly.

"You ready to go home?"

Flint's unexpected and coarse voice pulled her up short. How long had he been there? Had he heard Mary's offer? She swung around and met his gaze. As usual it gave nothing away. He leaned against the doorjamb as though he hadn't a care in the world. She knew better. Averting her gaze, she stood. "I'm ready when you are."

"Surely you don't have to go yet, Flint."

"'Fraid so, Mary. I've been up since four this morning mending fences and I'm still not finished."

"Ah, hell, don't pay her no mind," Ed put in, coming to stand beside Flint in the door. "She thinks the day doesn't begin till noon."

"That's a boldfaced lie, Ed Liscomb, and you know it."

Everyone laughed, then said their goodbyes.

"They're lovely people," Stephanie commented several minutes later, watching Flint's competent hands steer the truck down the drive.

"The best."

"I had . . . a great time. Thanks for taking me."

He turned toward her, and his gaze made a slow search of her face. "Were you ready to go home?"

Home. "Of course," she managed to whisper.

When he turned his attention back to the road, she closed her eyes, her thoughts reeling. Home. Her mind toyed with it. She found she liked the sound of it.

Too much.

Nine

Had she been at Flint's ranch for only a week? It seemed a lifetime. The last two days had been filled with nothing but emptiness. And frustration.

Something told Stephanie she was the type who stayed busy, worked hard and consciously prided herself on her ability to cope with any situation.

But she had nothing to do or look forward to save the passage of time, and this inactivity lowered her deeper and deeper into depressed loneliness. How long had it been since she'd laughed? Even the two trips back to Ed and Mary's had failed to lift her depression, although Flint's closest friends had done their best to boost her spirits.

The last time she'd gone into town with Flint to get supplies, she'd stocked up on magazines and paperback books. But soon she tired of reading, nor was she interested in the soaps.

And then there was Flint. While he went out of his way to see that she had everything she needed, he also went out of his way to avoid her.

He rarely joined her for any meal except dinner, which she prepared. She hadn't known if she could cook, but she found, to her delight, that she could. She knew he appreciated her endeavor as he always ate heartily before excusing himself and going to the cubbyhole off his bedroom that served as his office.

Twice, though, Flint had stayed to drink a cup of coffee. But his company had its drawbacks. His close proximity, the intimidating warmth of his body, his disturbing appraisal of her never failed to shatter her composure as no spoken words of his would have done.

Still, she would have preferred his presence, as unsettling as it was, to the loneliness. Today was falling into that same pattern as the other days, only this time she wasn't going to sit idly by. Things could not go on as they were. The time had come for her to take matters into her own hands and find out who she was.

She had made it a point to get up early in hopes of cornering Flint before he left to tend to his cattle. But again she'd been too late.

As she walked outside, the sun sparked the sky into changing panoramas of color. She paused and stared, then drew the clean morning air through her lungs. One could overdose on its freshness, she thought with a whimsical smile.

Shielding her eyes, she looked toward the barn, hoping she might get lucky and catch him this time.

He'd commented last night at the dinner table that he had several sacks of salt blocks he had to load onto his pickup.

"I'd like to help," she'd said before she thought.

His expression had given nothing away, but she sensed she'd shocked him.

"May I?"

The corners of his lips curled, and it wasn't an amusing smile. "You can't be serious."

"And just why not?" she snapped.

"Because the barn's hot and dirty and no place for a woman."

"You mean it's no place for me, don't you?"

His eyes traveled a reckless path down her body. "I wouldn't think slumming in the barn would appeal to you."

"You don't know what would appeal to me." She heard the pain in her voice. Dammit, why was she letting him get to her?

He stood abruptly, and when he did, his chair made a loud scraping sound on the worn floor. "You're right, I don't." With that he turned and stamped toward the door.

She'd stared after him, trembling. Then she blinked back the tears and cleared the table. Before she finished, she had broken two dishes.

She had planned to talk to him the previous evening, but after that less than amiable conversation, she'd put it off. Just as she forced that unpleasantness to the back of her mind, Flint walked out of the barn.

"Flint!" she called.

He swung around. "Yo."

"Wait, please. I want to talk to you."

He strode toward her, his stride impatient, like everything else about him. He had on dusty jeans, a blue shirt and battered Stetson, giving the term "working cowboy" new meaning.

Definitely he was a fine specimen. But the physical appearance was merely icing. His formidable presence would be felt no matter where he was or how he dressed. He simply radiated power.

By the time he reached her, her mouth was dry. Crazy or not, the attraction was there, potent and swift.

"What's up?" he asked without preamble, though his tone held none of the contempt from last evening.

"We need to talk."

He raised his eyebrows. "You're up kinda early, aren't you?"

"Boredom can do that to you."

She saw something in his eyes spark and knew her veiled sarcasm had struck a nerve. But then he grinned a mocking grin, while his eyes ran down her slender figure with blatant appreciation. "That so, huh?"

"I don't find this amusing," she said primly, feeling anger rise in her throat.

His face changed. "No, I guess you don't. But then I wouldn't know, never having been bored."

"Unfortunately I don't have that luxury," she said snidely.

"Come on, let's walk," he said without warning.

"All right." She cast him a sidelong glance, uncertain of his mood. "Can you spare the time away from work?"

"Would it make any difference?"

Her gaze clashed with his. "No."

His only response was the tightening of his jaw.

For a moment they walked in silence, each lost in their own thoughts.

When they reached a clump of pecan trees just inside a fenced pasture, he paused and leaned against one of them. "What's this all about? Mary?"

She frowned. "Mary?"

"Yeah, Mary. Didn't she ask you to stay with them?"

"Oh, you heard?"

"I heard." His tone was bleak. "So what are you going to do?"

"What . . . what do you want me to do?"

"For God's sake, Stephanie!"

"Does . . . does that mean you want me to go?"

"No, dammit. It doesn't!"

She sucked in a deep breath, and when she did, the scent of sweat, of cows, of flesh filled her lungs, drugging her. She was more aware of him than ever before.

He muttered a curse at the same time his eyes probed hers—as if he were trying to pull her inside him.

The air shook between them. Then a tiny sigh suddenly escaped through her lips and broke the spell. His eyes shuttered, and his face became blank.

"So if it's not about your leaving. . . ?" He sounded tired now and impatient.

"In spite of what the doctor said, I feel I need to do something to try to find out who I am."

"Have you thought about a private detective?"

She tossed her head as if to clear it. "No...but then I haven't been thinking rationally, either. That sounds logical, though."

"If you decide to go that route, let me know. I have connections."

Her face fell. "Sometimes I think I'm doomed to remain in this black void forever."

"You aren't."

"You sound so sure."

"I trust Abe," he said simply.

"So do I, but—"

"Are you still having...those nightmares?"

She circled her lips with her tongue, and once again their eyes connected. The night she had cried in his arms once again rose to the forefront of her mind. His thoughts mirrored hers, she knew, for his eyes darkened and his breath quickened.

"Sometimes," she said haltingly.

They looked at each other a moment longer, then Flint cleared his throat. "Can you make heads or tails of them?"

"Yes and no. Once I dreamed about the crash...dreamed there was a fire..."

"Go on," he urged.

"That's all," she insisted, weary with the strain of trying to recall. "That's why it's so frustrating. It's almost like it's there only it's not."

"Well, I see it as a good sign."

"Maybe. But in the meantime, I need something to occupy my mind."

"I told you I had to work." There was censure behind his words.

She lowered her eyes, conscious of the heat in her cheeks. "I know... it's just..."

"For starters, I guess you could play the P.I."

Her head came up, but before she could reply, he went on, "Remember you mentioned checking with the airlines." He shrugged. "And calling the jewelry stores. They're long shots I know..."

Her eyes came back to life. "I could make some calls myself, couldn't I?" she asked eagerly.

"I suppose you could, now that you're feeling better."

"I'm positive I could get a Houston directory from the library."

Flint leaned his head sideways and was quiet for a moment. "You're excited about this, aren't you?"

"I told you I'm about to go crazy without anything to do."

"Speaking of something to do," he said, "I've gotta get back to work." He pushed away from the tree. "What about you?"

Stephanie's features clouded as she envisioned the long, empty day ahead. "I guess I'll go for a walk."

He hesitated, then said, "Maybe... er... we could take in a movie in town tonight, if you'd like, that is."

Stephanie drew back in surprise, not sure she'd heard him correctly. But when she deciphered the expression on his face, she knew she had. He looked as though he'd rather be hung from the nearest tree than do what he'd suggested. Well, that was just too bad. This was one time he should've kept his mouth shut and didn't.

She broke into a sudden and radiant smile. "I'd like that. I'd like that a lot."

Long after he'd returned to his chores, she was still smiling.

Flint was in a bad mood. He couldn't believe he'd offered to take her to the movie. Again he cursed his careless tongue, taking his anger out on the pitchfork and bales of hay. He'd only moments before finished loading the pickup with salt blocks for distribution. Still uptight, he'd decided to stack the hay.

Shirtless, he jabbed the fork into the guts of the third bale and hoisted it atop another one. His muscles tensed and burned.

Maybe he should have encouraged her to go stay with the Liscombs. Flint didn't know how much more of this "togetherness" he could take. He'd thought Stephanie was too fragile to uproot, but now he wasn't so sure. Despite her lack of memory, she seemed more able to cope than he did.

He could see her now, in his mind's eye, standing next to him, the sunlight warming her white skin to a honey color, skin that was as smooth and flawless as a perfect diamond. He ached to touch her. It made him physically ill. And not because of his celibacy, either. He wanted *her*.

But that was not to be, and he knew it.

"Forget her, dammit! She's not worth it." The sound of his own voice seemed to calm him, and for a moment he mulled the situation over rationally, calling a spade a spade.

He had nothing to offer her, except a toss in the sack. Though she sometimes behaved with airs, and while that needled him, she deserved better than that.

And so did he. She'd just mess up his head even more than it was already.

He paused and dragged air through his scorched lungs, then wiped his forehead. The sweat-drenched rag was halfway back into his pocket when he heard the scream.

Fear seized him. His blood turned to ice water and froze his limbs. Then he heard it again. Dropping his pitchfork, Flint tore out of the barn.

Stephanie had no idea how long she'd been walking or where she was. Time, though, was of no importance. She had no reason to hurry back to the house. But at least she had something to look forward to—two things actually, helping to track her past and a trip to the movies.

She smiled. While she sensed ranch life was completely foreign to her, she was adapting well, she thought. If only Flint would let her do something to help him, she'd almost be content. She shook her head, thinking how crazy that sounded.

She knew the reason behind it. Flint. Her smile widened into a grin. She still couldn't believe he'd offered to take her to the movies. She'd bet anything he was choking on those words about now. He was definitely a most unpredictable man, which made him that much more exciting. And dangerous.

Stephanie's smile disappeared and she sighed. For someone in her predicament, the last thing she needed was the complication of an affair, especially with a man who was so different, so hard. Yet she believed that underneath the cold, sarcastic face the world saw, there lurked a heart that was desperately in need of love. He would never admit it, though. No one could ever get that close. Least of all her.

But when he looked at her with those smoldering eyes... She yanked her thoughts away from this enigma of a man and concentrated on her surroundings. She had wandered inside a pasture dotted with black cattle busy munching on grass and wildflowers.

Distant pines rose heavenward. Nearby were oaks and one lone cottonwood, though its trunk was twice the size of the oaks. Cattle grazed near a pond. Unpaintable beauty lurked everywhere. Stephanie simply stood without moving and took it all in. She bent and picked a bouquet of wildflowers while the wind gently whispered against her face.

She didn't notice the animal until she stood once again. Nestled amongst a stand of tall grass, a few yards in front of her, lay a baby calf.

"Oh, you precious baby, you," she cooed, inching forward carefully so as not to frighten it. Had she ever seen one so young? Somehow she thought not, except maybe in pictures.

Stephanie stopped within arm's length, squatted down and balanced one knee on the ground. His coat was as black as midnight, but that was all she had time to notice before the calf noticed her. Immediately, it shook and tried to stand. But its thin, lanky legs were so wobbly, it couldn't.

"I'm sorry, I didn't mean to scare you," she whispered.

Her soft tone, however, had no effect. The calf continued to tremble and stare at her through wary black eyes.

Stephanie had gotten to her feet with every intention of distancing herself from the animal when she heard an odd sound. Her head popped up and her mouth fell open. She was consumed with pure horror.

Galloping across the meadow at full speed and snorting through its nose was the biggest, blackest, ugliest looking cow that Stephanie was sure God had ever put on this earth. And the creature was heading toward her.

Stephanie couldn't think. She couldn't breathe. She couldn't *move*. Her body felt weighted down with lead, while she watched in a shocked stupor. What released her limbs from their paralysis, she never knew. She only knew that one minute she couldn't function and the next she was screaming, a blood-curdling scream. The unexpected noise seemed to incense the cow that much more. Its speed picked up.

Stephanie screamed again, but not before turning and running through the grass. "Oh, God, help me, please!" she muttered, afraid to turn around and afraid not to. But she knew she was not alone. The pounding of hooves was right behind her.

She ran as if her very life depended on it. In this instance, she knew it did.

Flint tore through the barn door and saw her. And the cow.

He took off running. He reached her the instant she rounded the huge oak. Wordlessly she flung herself into his outstretched arms. He held her shivering body close against his.

"Oh, Flint." She pulled back and gulped for so much as the tiniest breath. "Oh, thank God... thank..." Her voice failed her. But once she stopped gulping, she lifted soft and misty eyes to him.

That's when something snapped inside him. He was already shaken from the shock he had suffered when he thought she might be injured by the mother cow. But intoxicated by the feel of her against him, his fear took a new turn.

"Dammit, woman, you don't have the sense God gave a billy goat!"

Stephanie pulled her head back. The pulse at the base of her throat beat frantically. *"What?"* The word was barely audible.

"What the hell were you doing!"

The rough fury in his voice seemed to act as the catalyst that roused her from her dazed state. She shouted back, "I was looking and talking to a baby calf, that's what!"

"That's about the most asinine thing I've ever heard! You could've been killed!"

"Maybe that would have been the answer to my problems!"

"Great! That's really great."

"Will you stop yelling at me?"

"No! You should've known better."

Her breathing was as sharp as his, her temper hotter. "Well, I didn't! How was I to know that... that black *thing* would come after me?"

"Common damn sense for one thing!"

"Go to hell!"

He imprisoned her arms in his long fingers. They held that pose, their eyes engaged in battle, their breathing ragged.

"I'd watch my mouth if I were you."

"Let go of me," she rasped. Her eyes stabbed him like twin daggers.

"Not until you calm down and listen to reason."

"No!" She struggled to break his hold on her.

Anger beat through him. "Settle down, you little wildcat." But there was still no give to her.

"Let go of me!" she said again.

"Bygod will you just shut up?"

"No, I won't shut up!" she flared back. "You don't have any right to—"

He tightened his grip on her shoulders, lifted her off the ground and propelled her backward against the trunk of the tree. He anchored his arms on either side. His body became a barrier, and before she could utter so much as a whimpering sound, he lowered his head and took her lips.

Instantly his system went into shock as if he had accidentally touched a live wire.

When he pulled away for air, she said, "Flint... please..."

"Please what?" he countered hoarsely. "You've been wanting this as much as I have." He advanced his hips, deliberately letting her feel his burgeoning hardness, and after a brief pause felt her response.

"You like this, don't you?"

"Please...don't," she said in a voice that was softly unconvincing.

Knowing that she was his for the taking, Flint experienced a heady surge of confidence. It relieved his harsh expression and reshaped his lips into an agonizing smile while he rotated against her with a motion that was a blatant statement of intent.

"Oh...F-Flint," she moaned.

"I know." His voice sounded thick and shaky as he held himself rigidly against her, his need a tangible pressure building in his groin.

A moan slid past her lips at the same time he kissed her again, thrusting his tongue deeper and deeper into her mouth, wanting, needing, aching...

With the same urgency Flint had grabbed her, he released her. Then pulling fresh air through his scalded lungs, he turned his back and stepped away.

The hot sun beat down around them.

He hadn't allowed his iron control to slip in a long time, and the experience left him feeling vulnerable, exposed. Finally having regained a sliver of that control, Flint twisted back around and said, "Look, I—" His mouth snapped shut as he realized he was talking to himself.

Stephanie was already halfway to the house.

Ten

___

The buckskin gelding loped; horse and rider moved as one. Flint didn't rein to a slower pace until he reached the pond near the barn. While the gelding lapped the cool water, Flint rested an arm across the saddle horn and tried to shut off his thoughts.

The sun had long ago washed the sky a reddish gold and was now concentrated on the pine trees in the distance. He liked this time of the morning when he was alone with nature. Even after the horse stopped drinking, he still didn't move, completely absorbed in the silence.

Today he should jump another hurdle in further implementing the ideas he had picked up in Arkansas. The herd had already grown significantly. But there was still a long way to go before he could take the cattle to market and turn a profit.

He'd also made plans to start remodeling the barn. Miraculously, it hadn't come tumbling down on top of his head. Ed had volunteered to help, and Flint had taken him up on his offer. Both were anxious to get started.

All the things Flint had to do suddenly piled up in his mind until they assumed overwhelming proportions, but then he dismissed them. The tasks would get done.

He wished he could dismiss Stephanie from his mind as easily. His deep sigh shattered the silence. Lifting the reins, he nudged the animal in the side and aimed him toward the barn.

Last evening, following that scene in the pasture, he knew she had gone to great lengths to avoid him. He couldn't fault her as he would've done the same thing.

He'd doubted he could ever face her again after the stunt he'd pulled. He felt like a heel. He *was* a heel. He had taken advantage of her when she was most vulnerable, so he deserved the consequences. But in that brief, volatile moment, when he'd ground his heat against her softness and plundered her lips with his, he'd been in heaven. God, but she'd tasted so good, smelled so good, felt so good....

He'd been thinking that very thing when he'd walked into the kitchen at six o'clock this morning and had seen her sitting at the table....

Their eyes had locked instantly, and for a moment neither seemed capable of speaking.

Finally he'd cleared his throat and said, "I didn't expect you up so early."

She glanced away. "I couldn't sleep."

The dark circles under her eyes and the slight droop of her mouth proved she spoke the truth. Instead of those imperfections distracting from her beauty, however, they enhanced it, especially as the purple blouse turned her blue eyes to violet and her hair to jet black. Yet something tore at his throat. She looked so lost.

He cursed himself again before admitting, "I couldn't sleep either."

Silence surrounded them.

"Maybe I should take..."

He knew what she was going to say, and the thought made him ill. "Look, I know this doesn't excuse what I did, but it won't happen again," he said, damning himself again for his lack of control.

"I'm as much to blame as you." She spoke as if she were out of breath.

"No, you're not," he said savagely. "I was way out of line."

She hadn't argued. She had stood instead and offered to fix him some breakfast, which he'd declined. After filling his thermos with coffee, he'd hurried toward the door like the gutless coward he was. He hadn't slowed down until he'd reached the barn.

Now Flint realized nothing had been settled, merely postponed. He did not know how much longer he could go on like this. A demanding pressure built between his thighs as he thought about how much he wanted her, how much he wanted to suckle those nipples, bury his hardness inside her...

The emotions raging inside him were such that he didn't see Ed leaning against the entrance to the barn until he was almost on him. Flint pulled the gelding up short.

From under the brim of his hat, Ed stared at horse and rider and drawled, "'Bout time. I had all but given you up."

"What brings you over this early?" Flint asked, swinging out of the saddle.

Ed removed his hat, then scratched his head. "Thought we might get started on the barn."

"I'd like to, but there're a couple of cows in the south pasture that need attention. I just found them."

"Need any help?"

"Nah, but thanks for the offer."

"Anytime."

Flint shifted his gaze to the dilapidated structure and shook his head. "Maybe next week we can start tearing down the back side of this heap." He paused, lost in thought. "Think I'll ever get this place in good working order?"

"We both know what it takes. Time and money."

Using his Stetson, Flint slapped a patch of dirt off his thigh. "Time I got. Money I don't."

"You know how to remedy that."

Flint held up his hand. "Don't say it. I won't take your money, Ed. With what little I have left from Uncle Charlie and with what I've managed to save, I'll make it."

"You're about the stubbornest sonofabitch I know."

Flint grinned. "That so, huh?"

"That's so, and you know it."

Flint grinned again while he unsaddled the gelding and led it inside the barn.

Ed followed him, the cool dimness of the barn a welcome relief from the bright sunlight and April humidity.

"How're things going?" Ed asked casually.

Too casually, Flint thought, cutting his friend a hard glance. "They're fine."

"Hey, don't give me that. You got a burr up your butt about something."

Flint stiffened. "What makes you say that?"

"Don't know. Just a hunch."

"I wouldn't count on those hunches too much, if I were you."

Ed snorted, and when he did, his beer belly shook.

In spite of himself, Flint smiled. "You best lay off that stuff."

"What stuff?" Ed's face was innocent.

"You know what stuff. It's gonna kill you."

Ed rubbed his belly and smiled. "Ah, but what a way to go."

"I agree. I could use a couple of beers myself right now."

Ed's features sobered. "Sorry, I shouldn't . . ."

"No apology necessary."

"So is it your houseguest that's got you wishin' you could fall off the wagon?"

Flint's first reaction was to tell Ed to mind his own business, but he didn't. He knew that underneath that gruff talk, Ed was concerned. He'd told Ed shortly after they met about his bout with the bottle, because right off Ed had insisted he drink a beer with him.

"Okay, so she's a problem."

"Think she'll ever get her memory back?"

Flint grabbed a rag off the rickety table beside him and rubbed on the saddle. "I'm beginning to wonder."

"Damned shame." Ed's eyes twinkled. "She's sure a fine-looking woman."

Flint raised his head and glared at him.

Ed didn't flinch. "Yeah. Now, I couldn't be cooped up with her, and—"

"You've made your point." Flint's tone was testy at best.

Ed chuckled. "Yeah, I guess I have at that." He paused. "Wanna join the womenfolk for a cup of coffee?"

"You mean Mary's with you?"

"As we speak, she's inside talking to Stephanie."

"What about?" Was Mary trying to persuade Stephanie into coming to their house? He ground his teeth together.

"The dance we're having at our place."

Flint felt relief on one hand, but new suspicions were roused on the other. "I hope you're not getting at what I think you are. You know I don't want any part—"

"Well, something tells me that's about to change."

This time Flint snorted. "No way."

"We'll see." Ed chuckled knowingly. "Come on, let's go get that coffee."

Stephanie cradled her banging head in her hands and prayed for relief. None came. Besides suffering another nightmare during the night, her mind reeled from the confrontation with Flint.

Earlier, she had stumbled into the bathroom at the end of the hall, and after filling a cup with water, had swallowed two of the pills prescribed by Abe. She had gone back to bed and told herself she needed the sleep after her ordeal. In reality, she knew she was postponing facing her conscience for her part in yesterday's debacle.

Now, as she dressed, the scene paraded before her mind in living color and added to her confusion. How could she have behaved so wantonly? She might as well have let him rip her clothes off and make love to her on the spot.

What had come over her?

At first she had blamed her actions on her condition, on the fear and uncertainty that hovered over her like a dark cloud. That was part of it, sure. But that wasn't all. In his arms she had felt alive, captivated by everything that was happening to her, as if his mouth, his hands, his strong arms were guiding her.

She should be ashamed. She *was* ashamed. Yet she hadn't wanted him to stop. And that had scared her, made her run.

To make matters worse, when she saw him earlier in the kitchen, she had wanted to fling herself back into his arms. Should she leave? Go to Mary's? Logic said yes while her heart balked.

"What a mess," she moaned, before standing and hustling to the cabinet. Just as she raised the coffeepot, something bright outside caught her attention. She looked through the window; Ed's pickup filled her vision. Both doors opened, and Ed and Mary hopped out.

Stephanie moaned again. While she enjoyed Mary's company, now was not a good time. Not only did she feel terrible, she looked terrible, which was bound to bring on questions she wouldn't want to answer. But short of being rude, she had no choice but to be sociable as Mary was headed toward the house while Ed went toward the barn.

Five minutes later Mary sat at the table in front of her, sipping coffee and chattering nonstop.

"I hope you don't mind my crashing in on you this early, but Ed thought maybe Flint might like to get started on his barn."

"That's fine. I was about to get started making calls." Though she tried to keep the edge out of her voice, she couldn't.

"You're becoming more frustrated by the day, aren't you, dear?"

"I'm afraid so."

Mary reached across the table and squeezed Stephanie's hand. "Maybe you're trying too hard, not giving yourself enough time. It's only been...what, a week, week and a half?"

"Thereabouts, but it seems like forever."

"Well, the way I see it, a party is what you need."

Stephanie wrinkled her brows. "A party."

"Uh-huh. Our dance club's monthly social is at our place, and it's going to be a big shindig."

"I'm sure."

"We'd love for you to come."

The thought of moving with Flint in time to the music... Alarm flared in Stephanie's eyes. "Oh, no, I couldn't."

"You don't have to dance, not if you don't want to. There's tons of other stuff to do."

"Such as?"

Mary laughed. "Eat."

"Mmm, that sounds good."

"I'm glad to hear you say that. You can certainly use a few pounds."

"You sound like Flint."

Mary gave her a strange look, but whatever was on her mind, she didn't say, much to Stephanie's profound relief. She wasn't up to the third degree today, concerning her and Flint's unorthodox relationship.

"In addition to a barbecue," Mary said, "there'll be fried catfish, hush puppies and fries."

Stephanie drew back in surprise. "Jeez, how many are y'all feeding? The five thousand?"

"Actually, it's just a handful. Our club's small." Mary's smile widened. "But those who do come eat like they've been felling trees."

"Sounds like fun." Stephanie's tone was whimsical.

"So come. You and Flint."

"Oh, no, I don't think..." Though her voice failed her, her mind did not. The possible consequences of dancing with Flint, being held against his rock-hard body, moving in time to music, didn't bear thinking about.

"I was hoping you'd be receptive and talk Flint into it." Mary sounded disappointed. "As we both know, he's a hard nut to crack. Ever since he came here, we've been trying to get him to join our club so that he could meet his neighbors. But he's flatly refused, and we haven't been able to budge him yet."

"I'm not surprised."

"I'm not either, but that doesn't mean it has to stay that way. Besides, it would do you good. It just might put a little color back in your cheeks.

"Well... I'll think about it. Only I can't, *won't* speak for Flint."

"Great. In the meantime, why don't you go shopping with me? I have scads of things to buy, even though I'm having it catered. I could use the company and you the change of scenery. Right?"

Stephanie's face brightened, only to then dim. "I really should start calling—"

"Ah, come on."

Stephanie felt pulled two ways. While she felt the urgent need to try to find out who she was, she wanted to take it easy. The latter seemed to be the most pressing. "All right, you win," Stephanie said, suppressing a sigh.

"You ladies mind sharing some coffee with us?"

Both Stephanie and Mary, caught unaware, swung around and watched as Flint and Ed strode across the threshold.

Mary had eyes only for Flint. "Guess what Stephanie and I have been discussing?"

"The dance." Flint's tone was dry as parchment.

"And she's agreed to come and bring you with her."

Eleven

————

"Well, what d'you think? You having a good time?"

Stephanie smiled at Ed, who was busy stroking his full beard. "The party's wonderful."

"Ah, come on now. You being from the city, you must've been to lots of shindigs like this."

Stephanie winced visibly.

"Sorry," Ed said awkwardly, "I forget..."

"Don't apologize." She forced a bright smile. "I'm sure you're right."

Ed squeezed her shoulders. "You have a good time now, you hear. If you need anything, you just holler." He paused and aimed his gaze toward Flint. "Why don't you go ask that sour-faced fellow to dance?" He grinned, then winked. "Just might loosen him up."

Flint was propped against a tree, near the table laden with goodies.

Stephanie's lips twitched. "I think I'd rather take my chances on stepping in front of a Mack truck."

Ed threw back his head and laughed. "I'll have to hand it to you, you got his number." He paused again. "So, are you?"

"What?" she asked innocently, but she knew what he was getting at.

"You know what. Ask him to dance."

"No."

"I dare you," Ed challenged, his whiskey-edged voice deepening.

She smiled with syrupy sweetness. "The answer's still no."

"Oh, heck." He grinned and snapped his fingers. "I sure had you figured for a gambler."

Stephanie merely laughed.

"Well, since there's not gonna be any fireworks, I guess I'd better circulate. Orders from my old lady. Will you be all right?"

"I'll be fine. I was on my way to help Mary, anyway."

"See you later."

Stephanie nodded vaguely, having already turned her attention back to Flint, who continued to lounge against the tree, his Stetson hiding his eyes. As usual, he looked mouth-wateringly sexy, dressed in a pair of pressed jeans, polished boots and white chambray shirt that accentuated his tan. He affected her despite her efforts not to let him.

Again the thought of dancing with him did strange things to her body. Her heart raced, and her palms sweated. But she was wasting good energy. He wasn't about to dance with her or anyone else. His boorish attitude left no doubt that he'd rather be anywhere but there.

And she found it hard to believe that he actually was. She'd have to give Mary credit; she had pulled a fast one. When Mary had announced that she, Stephanie, had consented for both of them, Flint had glowered at her....

"Did you tell her that?"

Stephanie licked her lips while wanting to strangle Mary. "Actually, I—"

Mary cut in. "Now, Flint, don't go getting—"

"Oh, what the hell," he barked. "We might as well go and get it over with."

Mary's expression turned incredulous. "Did you hear that, Ed?"

"Sure did, honey. And we'll hold him to that, even if I have to hog-tie him."

"That'll be the day," Flint countered with the beginnings of a smile on his lips.

His sudden good humor hadn't fooled Stephanie. Something told her that if their eyes were to collide again, she would see a murderous glint reflected in his.

He hadn't mentioned the party, however, until this morning when he'd told her to be ready by six.

Now, as she pulled her gaze from him, Stephanie smothered a sigh and made her way toward the side entrance to the house. The night couldn't have been lovelier, she thought as she meandered through the tables set up on the grounds.

The air smelled fresh and sweet. Stars littered the sky. Lanterns hung from trees and posts surrounding a portable dance floor in the middle of the huge yard. A band and singer crooned the latest country-western ballad while dancers, wrapped tightly in one another's arms, swayed to the music.

When she and Flint had arrived, the party had been in full swing. Mary had met them when they rounded the corner and introduced Stephanie to the other couples. She was welcomed immediately, though she couldn't help but notice that Flint was the one who garnered the most attention from several unattached females.

Mary had then insisted they take advantage of the food, which was displayed with the same skill and decorative taste as everything else. Barbecue, catfish and Mexican food—tacos, chicken and beef *fajitas*— crowded the long table. Stephanie had chosen a little of each while Flint had chosen a lot of each.

She'd been in a festive mood as Flint had actually talked to her on the way, explaining about his cattle and the progress he'd made with them. He'd also told her about the calf he expected to be born soon.

The days preceding the party hadn't been too bad, either. He'd actually taken her riding and had let her watch him and a hired hand, Smitty, work on the barn. She'd been their gofer.

But once they had reached the party, his mood had changed. Now, however, she knew it had not changed for the better. He hadn't wanted to come, and he made sure everyone knew it.

That thought was still uppermost in Stephanie's mind when she entered the kitchen, only to suddenly stop. Instead of stepping into Mary's kitchen, another one flashed in front of her eyes, one with bright oranges and yellows. *Her kitchen?* She blinked several times until the vision cleared.

"Stephanie, honey," Mary cried, "what on earth? You look like you've just seen a ghost."

"Perhaps I have—my past."

Mary set down a bowl of potato salad and grasped one of Stephanie's hands. "Here, sit down. You're not making sense."

"Yes, I am," she said excitedly, sinking into the chair, her face no longer ashen. "When I walked in here, a picture of my kitchen swam before my eyes. I could see every detail so clearly."

Mary clapped her hands. "Why, that's wonderful news. Have you mentioned that to Flint?"

"No, not yet."

"Are you going to?"

"Yes, but right now I'm going to ask him to dance." Once the words left her mouth, Stephanie was stunned by them. Then recovering, she said breathlessly, "Ed dared me, you know." Was it the dare that prompted such madness on her part, a madness she couldn't even put a name to?

Mary laughed. "Good luck. Better you than me."

"For heaven's sake, I won't bite."

"Are you sure?" he drawled.

Stephanie had found Flint swaggering toward the table where a huge urn of iced tea sat. Before he could refill his cup, she'd approached him.

Now, as he peered down at her with a scowl on his face, she didn't know whether to curse him or hit him.

"Jerk," she muttered under her breath.

He heard her, though, and chuckled. "I've been called worse."

Color mounted in her face, but she didn't back down. "I'm not surprised."

He simply looked at her for a long moment, then in a rough voice said, "Come on."

The platform was packed, but that didn't stop Flint from pulling her onto the floor and drawing her into his arms. Still she hadn't expected to feel the heavy crush of his hard body against hers, nor have his arms clamp around her with such force.

Tension stretched her nerves despite her attempts to relax. And the scent of his warm skin didn't help any, especially as her mouth pressed against the open vee of his shirt. She wet her lips and ached to stroke that vulnerable spot with the tip of her tongue. She blew warm air there instead.

"God, Stephanie!" he grated into her hair at the same time she felt his involuntary arousal. But Stephanie was too engrossed in her own reaction to move away, feeling as if something had burst inside her, exposing forces far too strong to contain. She felt plugged in to a new high and began to move sensuously against him in time to the music.

"What the hell do you think you're doing!" The words sounded tortured, but he didn't push her away. Instead, he tightened his hold and followed her lead.

His chin grazed her hair along with the heated draught of his breath. A slight tilt of her head and their lips would meet. The thought was not just a heady temptation, but an exciting ache as she knew he wouldn't be able to resist her.

But the memory of that other time brought her abruptly to her senses. This was not a game to Flint.

He was not a man to be toyed with. With a gulp she pulled herself together and stiffened in his arms.

He thrust her to arm's length, his dark eyes expressionless. When he spoke, his voice still didn't sound like his own.

"Are you ready to go?"

"Yes."

Five minutes later they left.

"There's something I want to ask you."

They were halfway to the ranch, and this was the first time either of them had spoken. They were too shaken and too wary after what had just happened on the dance floor to say much of anything.

"All...right," Stephanie said.

Without warning, he swung the truck off the highway onto the grassy shoulder.

Her eyes widened. "What are you doing?"

"What does it look like I'm doing?"

"Stopping."

He didn't respond.

"But...why?"

"To take care of a little unfinished business."

"I...I don't understand."

"You will."

She had just parted her lips to say more, when he reached out and pulled her toward him. His voice against her lips came out tight and clogged. "Ever since the other night, I've been wanting this and now tonight..."

"Don't talk," she breathed. Her hands, which seconds before had been idle, crawled behind his neck and threaded through his thick hair. "Just kiss me."

She felt him hesitate as if he were having second thoughts, and her senses clamored in frustration. But then, with a groan, he found her lips with greedy accuracy.

Clinging to him, she gave in to the searing heat of his mouth, the hungry invasion of his tongue. She twisted in his arms so that her throbbing breasts were embedded in the ungiving wall of his chest. The flesh between her thighs came alive, and her stomach plummeted as if on a descending elevator. She knew this was insane, but she wanted him. How she wanted him.

As before and equally as sudden, he jerked his lips from hers, his breathing erratic.

"Flint..."

"Don't look at me like that," he said in a strangled tone.

"I...don't understand. You..." She couldn't go on, feeling sick.

"Surely you know it's stop now or not at all! And I don't think you want me to take you here in the front seat of this truck like two animals in heat."

His words assaulted her like a fist to the stomach. She drew back and tried to say something. But there was no need; her grieving eyes spoke for her.

He turned away as if he couldn't bear what he saw there. "Believe me, you'll thank me for this later."

While the inside of the truck was silent, sounds of the night throbbed around them. Crickets chirped. Katydids cried. The wind howled.

The longer they remained silent, the more the tension mounted. Stephanie was aware of him beside her with every beat of her heart. And despite his coldness, her nerves were on fire. On fire for him. Closing her eyes, she inhaled his scent. She ached to touch him. Again.

Instead she stole a glance at him. He was watching her. A muscle ticked overtime in his jaw. She had to relieve the explosive silence or scream.

"What . . . did you want to ask me?"

"I want to take you up in Ed's small plane."

She didn't know what she expected, but it hadn't been this. "No," she said flatly, fear thickening her tongue.

"You need to fly again and so do I. Besides, I thought it might help trigger your memory."

"You hate yourself for . . . wanting me, don't you?"

If the sudden change of subject stunned him, he failed to show it. His eyes didn't flicker as they made a slow search of her face. "Yes, dammit, I do."

She bit down on her lip to keep from crying. And for the longest time they listened as the silence once again hung heavy over them.

Finally Stephanie turned to him and said, "All right, you win. I'll go up with you in the plane."

He faced her again. "What made you change your mind?"

"The sooner I get my memory back, the sooner I can leave."

"And you can't wait, can you?"

All at once her voice betrayed her. It quavered. Without warning, tears trickled down her face. "Only because that's what *you* want."

He looked at her as if he were going to grab her again, longing intense on his face. It took her breath away.

But instead of touching her, he let loose a string of colorful expletives, cranked the truck and spun back onto the road.

Twelve

The sky was perfect. It reminded Stephanie of a sapphire that had been polished to its gleaming best. She could reach out and touch it; she just knew she could. But she was too frightened to try.

So she remained strapped in the seat of the noisy little plane with her heart lodged in the back of her throat. It threatened to choke her each time Flint so much as moved the yoke.

She had been positive she wouldn't be able to set one foot inside this ugly machine—and not because of the previous crash. That was still a blank in her mind. But when Flint came to assist her inside, a nameless fear deep inside her rendered her stiff-legged.

"You're having second thoughts, aren't you?"

She nodded.

Wind caught his hair and tossed it around. She watched a loose strand tickle his forehead. "It's your call," he said.

Stephanie licked her parched lips. "Let's do it."

They were airborne several minutes before he looked at her and commented, "That wasn't too bad now, was it?"

"Yes," she whispered, biting down on her lower lip to keep her teeth from chattering.

His eyes registered concern. "You aren't going to be sick, are you?"

"No...no I don't think so."

"I don't suppose you could look down. The trees and wildflowers are something to see."

She wet her lips. "I'm...I'm sure they are, but if it's all the same to you, I'd rather see them from ground level."

"Is anything coming back to you?" Flint asked after a moment.

"No," she said, and rested her eyes on him. That was when she noticed the white line around his mouth. How could she have been so insensitive? Flint had gone through the same nightmare as she had, maybe even worse because he was conscious throughout the horrifying ordeal. "What about you? Are you okay?"

"I was a bit shaky at first, but I'm fine now."

"If only something would jar loose in my memory..." She paused and tried to push back the despair playing havoc with her inside, but to no avail. She felt like crying.

"You'd best stop punishing yourself, or you're never going to remember."

Flint brought the Cessna back in for a safe landing, sensing she'd had enough. By the time her feet were on the ground, Stephanie was near tears.

"Are you sure you're all right?" Flint's gaze bored into her.

"No, I'm not sure about anything."

"When we get home, you should lie down for a while."

"What about Ed and Mary?" Out of the corner of her eye, Stephanie saw the Liscombs making their way toward the plane.

"They'll understand. You go ahead and get in the truck. I'll explain to them."

Stephanie flashed him a grateful smile.

He looked at her for a long moment, then turned toward Ed and Mary.

Her mind seemed a dark and gaping hole; too many thoughts battled for air. Was she dreaming again? She moaned, tossed the covers back, rolled from one side of the bed to the other. What was wrong? What was happening to her? She had to be dreaming...about the crash...about Flint...about the plane ride...

The moan came out a wail. She shot up in the bed, clutched the sheet to her naked breasts while her eyes jumped wildly around the room.

"Oh, my God," she whispered.

"If there's nothing else, I'll be on my way."

Flint nodded at Smitty Williams, the slender, wiry man who was thankful for the chance to work, even if it was only part-time. "That about covers it for now."

"Will you be wantin' to do some brandin' next week?" Smitty asked after he had limped to the barn door.

"Hope so," Flint said, rubbing the back of his neck. "But I can't say for sure. Ed's been on my tail to get started on this pile of crap."

"Well, just holler when you need me again."

"You take care of that leg now, you hear."

Smitty waved his hand. "Will do."

Alone, Flint mopped his brow, then gathered his tools. The front pasture gate was broken and had to be repaired before some of his herd got loose. He could have let Smitty fix it, but he wanted—*needed*—to do it himself, though Lord knows, he had more than enough to do already. Still, manual labor was his best mental therapy.

Stephanie. Forever Stephanie. That slender, black-haired witch had invaded his life and turned it upside down. Half the time he couldn't think straight, he ached for her so much.

But he wasn't about to give in and indulge himself. He'd made the mistake of touching her once too often as it was. To do so again would be inviting self-destruction. So far he'd risen to the challenge.

It'd been hard, though, especially this morning when he'd taken Stephanie up in the plane. He'd watched her face turn red, then white, then gray. He'd had to quell the urge to pull her into his arms and assure her everything was going to be all right.

Even afterward when he'd seen the fear, the uncertainty still reflected in her eyes, before she walked into her room and closed the door, he still hadn't given in to his urges.

Flint's hand suddenly stilled, as did his thoughts. A gusty breath from the edge of the woods brought him around. A doe stood poised and stared at him, defiance in every line of its young body. The animal repeated the strange sound, then bucked its head as if to show its disapproval of Flint's presence so close to its domain. Before Flint could react, it darted through the trees.

A brief smile touched his lips as he set about his task. He yanked off a rotten piece of wood, only to drop it.

"Sonofabitch," he muttered, lifting a finger to his lips, but not until he pulled out a sliver of wood with his teeth. When the bleeding stopped, he picked up his hammer and battered the remaining wood until it lay in a rubble at his feet.

"Long time no see, good buddy."

Flint whirled around, then lunged to his feet. "Why you ol' sonofagun, you! Haven't you learned yet you can get your head blown off for sneaking up on someone like that!"

Lee Holt, his friend and ex-partner at the agency, cocked his head to one side and grinned. "Not without a gun they won't," he drawled.

Flint returned the grin and extended his hand to the tall, sandy-haired man sporting wire-rim glasses across his nose. They made him look more like an English professor than a drug agent. But looks were deceiving. He was a sharp-witted, tough and highly skilled agent.

And he was the only man who Flint would trust with his life. In job-related incidents, they had been through hell and back and that made for a special friendship.

"What brings you to this neck of the woods?"

Lee shoved his glasses farther up on his nose. "Guess I wanted to see for myself that you were in one piece after that crash."

"Well, as you can see, I am."

"Anyway, didn't I warn you I'd show up on your doorstep one of these days?"

"Yep, but I didn't believe you."

"My grandmother lives in Lufkin, remember?"

"Ah, that's right." Flint removed his hat and again wiped his brow. "You want some tea or Coke?" Flint paused. "You know I don't keep any beer..."

"I was hoping that was still the case," Lee said, casually stuffing his hands into the pocket of his slacks and scrutinizing Flint closely.

Flint changed the subject. "You on vacation?"

"Sort of." Lee shifted his gaze.

"What does that mean?"

"Let's walk. You can give me the grand tour."

"Look, Lee," Flint began, his suspicions growing, "if you're really here about—"

"Hey, lighten up, will ya."

Flint scowled.

They walked only a few steps when Lee stopped. "You sure you're okay? I mean you sure that crash didn't..."

"What makes you think that?"

"Could be because you're up to your butt in alligators."

Flint's features turned cynical. "You always did have a way with words, Holt."

"I try," Lee responded with a grin. Then it faded, and his expression sobered. "I saw the way you were attacking that wood as if it was one of the thugs dealing drugs."

"Don't remind me."

"Hey, partner," he said, "seems to me like you're still nursing one helluva sore inside you. If you don't take some good medicine mighty soon, you'll up and die of blood poison."

"And you think coming back to that stink hole is the right medicine?"

"Yeah, as a matter of fact I do. Best I can tell, ranch life hasn't improved your disposition one iota or your outlook on life."

"It had up until a few days ago."

"So what happened?"

"There's someone...er...staying with me."

Lee's mouth fell open. "You have a houseguest? Now, that's a crock."

"Shut up," Flint grumbled darkly.

Lee grinned. "A woman."

"Yes."

"Well, that's been known to put some pep in ye ol' gumbo."

Again Flint scowled. "When did you get to be such a comedian?"

Lee's eyes narrowed, and the humor fled. "Lots of things have changed since you've been gone."

"If it's all the same to you, I'd rather not hear about them, either."

Lee shrugged. "Okay."

Flint wasn't fooled. He knew he wasn't going to get off the hook that easily. Lee was here for a reason, and

Flint knew he wouldn't leave until he unburdened himself. Lee was just biding his time and humoring him.

"So how did you come by your houseguest?"

Flint gave him a thumbnail account of the accident and Stephanie's plight, deleting only the personal aspects of the traumatic situation.

"That's something, man," Lee said, shaking his head. "In case you don't already know it, I'm glad you're safe."

"That's comforting to know," Flint's tone dripped with sarcasm.

"I guess that's why we work so well together, huh?"

"Worked. Past tense. *Comprende?*"

Again Lee shrugged. "So tell me about her?"

"I already have."

"No, you haven't."

Flint didn't say anything.

"I thought you wanted off that ferris wheel for good, my friend."

"If you're referring to a wife, two point three children and the house in the suburbs with the white picket fence around it, you're right."

Lee scooped a lock of hair off his forehead. "Then come back to work."

"Are you outta your mind?"

"You haven't resigned yet, Flint."

"Only because I haven't had time."

Lee sank against the nearest tree. "Dammit, man, you can't. The agency needs you. *I* need you. I've had three partners since you left, and I swear none of 'em had enough brains to fill a thimble."

Flint grinned. "You don't say?"

"Aw, man, I'm serious."

"So am I." Flint looked off in the distance. "I like it here. This land is gonna heal me."

Lee sneered. "You can't be serious about this cowboy game?"

"Well, I am," Flint said flatly.

"Just say you'll think about it."

"I'll think about it, only because I owe you."

"That's all I'm asking," Lee said, slapping Flint on the back. "Come on, show me this ninth wonder of the world."

"How long you planning to hang around?" Flint asked.

Following the tour, he and Lee had wandered back to where Lee's car was parked. Lee was inside his car, and Flint's elbows were bent on the vinyl top. He peered inside.

"A couple more days."

"I guess your grandmother's glad to see you."

"Yeah." Lee grinned and rubbed his stomach. "She's been puttin' the groceries on the table."

"That's obvious," Flint said, and dropped his gaze to his friend's protruding stomach. Before Lee could make a suitable comeback, he added, "Are you planning to stop by again?"

Lee grinned. "Are you kiddin'? I wouldn't miss meeting this lady for anything."

"Who said you were going to meet her?"

"Did I ever tell you you're a real pain in the butt, Carson?"

"Every day we worked together," Flint said drolly.

"Well, I haven't changed my mind."

Flint grinned a lop-sided grin and slammed his hand against the car door. "Go on. Get outta here before I give you something to whine about."

He watched in silence as Lee cranked his car, backed up, then spun his tires. Dust rose and clogged Flint's nostrils and throat. "Hey, you bastard, I'll get you for that!"

"Flint?"

At the sound of Stephanie's voice, he whipped around. For a moment he treated himself to a slow perusal of her. He assumed she had just awakened as her jeans and shirt were rumpled, even askew. And her eyes had a slightly glazed look. Nevertheless, with the wealth of her black hair in careless disorder, she made a picture that would stay with him for a long time.

He cleared his throat and stepped closer. That was when he noticed how pale she was. "Is something wrong? You look like you've just seen a ghost."

She shook her head so that her hair brushed her cheek. "Actually, I think I've just laid them to rest."

He frowned. "Care to explain that?"

Her delicately drawn features went curiously still, and she didn't say anything.

"Stephanie," he prodded, searching her face.

Through the concealing thickness of her lashes, she looked at him and smiled tremulously. "My memory has returned."

Thirteen

The statement ripped through him like a dull blade. Yet he kept his face impassive.

"So you finally know who you are."

"I can't believe it, but it happened just like Abe said it would." Stephanie's voice held awe, and her eyes were wide, as if she couldn't believe the sudden turn of events.

"Why don't we go sit on the porch?" Flint suggested abruptly.

Stephanie perched on the edge of the swing, and Flint leaned against a post.

"So when did things fall into place?" he asked, sifting through his feelings and not liking any of them. Why was he overreacting? He should be relieved she had opened that dark chapter in her life. And he was. Only...

"Just...now, actually," she said. "I...woke up from my nap, and everything was there."

His chest swelled as he drew air deep into his lungs and braced himself. "Everything?"

"Everything." She didn't so much as flinch under his direct gaze. "Even our less than amicable conversation on the plane."

A sickly sun peered through the now overcast sky while the silence built.

"But I don't hold that against you," she added in a breathy rush. "Especially after all you've done for me."

"Forget it."

She rejected that with an impatient toss of her head. "I have no intention of forgetting it."

"So what's next?"

"Notify my family, of course."

"And who is that?"

"My mother. If she's back from Europe."

"So that accounts for why she hasn't tracked you down."

"She didn't even know I was going to Arkansas."

"What about your dad?"

"He's...dead, and I'm an only child." She paused and took a steadying breath. "But I have to notify Kathy Gentry, who runs my shop."

"She didn't know your travel plans either, I take it."

"No. She knew I was going to check several sources, but she didn't know I was going to Arkansas."

"If only you'd told me the name of your business, much of this mess could've been avoided."

"It's Collections by Stephanie."

His head moved in the briefest of nods. "What about the man at the airport? Who was he?"

"David Weston."

"Go on."

Her white upper teeth imprisoned her lower lip for a moment. "He's my ex-fiancé, actually."

"So what's he to you now?" he asked tersely, shocked by the things he felt.

Without hesitation, she explained in detail about his aunt's jewelry.

"Someone oughta teach that creep a lesson." There was a hard set to Flint's jaw.

"He's harmless, really. It's just that he doesn't like being told no."

"Sounds like someone I know," he said, more for his own benefit than hers.

"Are you referring to your visitor?"

His eyes settled for a moment on the gentle swell of her breasts. "Yeah," he said tightly, his eyes flickering.

"Is he a . . . friend?"

"A friend and my ex-partner."

"He's trying to get you to return, isn't he?"

"How did you know?"

She shrugged. "I didn't, I just guessed. So what are you going to do?"

"I don't know. But I don't want to talk about me right now."

She eased back in the swing and didn't say anything.

"So when are you leaving?"

"Actually, I was thinking I might stay a while longer." Her smile was fragile. "If you don't mind, that is."

Shocked silence greeted her words. Flint couldn't respond even if he'd wanted to. He was too busy grappling with his own emotions. Logic told him she would eventually regain her memory. Yet he hadn't been prepared for it.

But neither had he been prepared for the bombshell she just dropped, having convinced himself that once she reclaimed her identity, she'd be out of his house and life forever. Only now she asked to stay. Suddenly everything was more tangled than ever.

She should leave. That was the sane recourse. Every day the ache for her grew worse. It was all he could do not to touch her, while savoring what it would be like to do just that, to taste her skin, feel her nipples come to life under his tongue...

In the backwash of those emotions, nausea washed through him. Yet the thought of her leaving was unbearable even though she stirred feelings he didn't want to face.

"Flint?"

"Do you think that's wise?" His expression was that of a man in torment.

Her mouth etched into a weak smile. "Probably not, but if I promise not to bother you..."

"That's not the point, and you know it."

"Just for a few more days, that's all I'm asking."

"Why?"

"I...I was planning to put some distance between David and myself by visiting a friend in Austin..."

"So you figure this is as good a place as any to hide?" For a second he had thought she wanted to stay because she cared.... Fool, he diagnosed grimly, his heart twisting at the pain she never failed to arouse in him.

"Something like that."

He stared at her and then turned away, shoving back his hair with a restless hand.

"Please."

He swung around, but instead of saying anything, he stared at her while his heart pounded in his chest.

"I could help you repair the barn," she said in a voice tinged with huskiness.

A slow smile spread from his lips to his eyes, kindling small fires. "Yeah, I guess you could at that."

"Thanks for everything, Mary."

The older woman grinned. "Don't thank me, I'm the one who had a good time. It's comforting to know someone can out-shop me."

Mary had just helped her unload several armloads of packages and was now back in her car, ready to head home.

Stephanie peered down at her and laughed sheepishly. "I did go overboard, didn't I?"

"Not at all. If you've got it, why not flaunt it." Mary's eyes turned serious. "By the way, welcome back to the real world, my dear."

Sudden tears clouded Stephanie's vision. "Thanks, Mary. Believe me, it's good to be back."

Two days had passed since her memory had returned. So far, things had gone smoothly. But then, she'd seen very little of Flint. They had both been too busy—Flint with his cattle and other chores and she with reacquainting herself with her life and responsibilities.

Following a long and traumatic talk with her mother, during which Flora had insisted she leave "that godforsaken place immediately" and return to Houston, Stephanie called Kathy. That conversation had been much more pleasant. She'd learned that things on the business front were fine, though Kathy had gone into hysterics when Stephanie informed her of what she'd been through.

Having taken care of those heart-wrenching duties, Stephanie had gone into town and wired her bank for money. Then she'd visited Ed and Mary. That was when she and Mary had planned this shopping expedition.

"How much longer do you plan to stay?" Mary asked, bridging the short silence.

Stephanie's good humor waned. "A ... few more days. I have to get back to work."

"We'll miss you."

"I'll miss you, too."

Mary laughed. "Well, there's no point in getting all maudlin now. You haven't gone yet."

"That's right, I haven't." She squeezed Mary's shoulder. "Thanks again. I'll talk to you later."

The minute she walked back into the house and eyed her purchases, her heart filled with excitement. She couldn't wait for Flint to come in so that she could show him what she'd bought. Glancing at her watch, she saw it was already five o'clock. If she was going to prepare a steak dinner as planned, she would have to hurry.

But instead of making her way toward the kitchen, she plopped down on the couch and opened the packages. She spread the items on the couch and two chairs.

"You did good, Stephanie Marsh," she said aloud with a broad smile. "Yes, ma'am, you did good."

Displayed in front of her were two colorful bedspreads as well as sheets, towels, glassware and pictures for the house. Spaced across the back of the couch were several shirts for Flint.

She didn't feel guilty about spending the money, either. That was the least she could do as Flint had saved her sanity, if not her life. She was aware that buying him things could in no way repay him, but nonetheless, it was something she wanted to do.

Besides, she wanted to leave something of herself behind. Abruptly, like a dark cloud dims the bright sun, the joy went out of her. When she thought about leaving, she always reacted like this. Yet she should have left two days ago.

Sure, she'd wanted a reprieve from David and his harassment, but that was only a smoke screen. She couldn't stand the thought of leaving Flint, which was ludicrous in itself. They were as different as two people could ever be. And even if they weren't, they had no future.

Flint Carson was not about to commit himself to a woman, least of all to her. And she didn't want him to, did she? Of course not. She was satisfied with her life and was eager to get on with it. But there was the unvarnished truth she could no longer deny: she was totally and completely under Flint's spell.

Thrusting these unsettling thoughts aside, she rushed into the bedroom and changed into a white jumpsuit she'd just bought. Satisfied that she looked her best, she made her way into the kitchen.

She had the steaks, baked potatoes and salad prepared with the coming of twilight. Only after she heard Flint shout his thanks to Ed for helping him in the pasture did she develop a case of the jitters.

"Cool it," she muttered, and hurried into the living room where she backed calmly against the mantel. Still, when she heard Flint rattle the front door knob, she almost jumped out of her skin.

"Stephanie?"

"In here."

He appeared in the doorway, and their eyes met. The connection between them was palpable. Her eyes dipped to his chest. His sweat-drenched shirt was unbuttoned to his navel. She felt her insides shake with wild heat.

His eyes darkened, as if he could read her thoughts, and he took one slow step toward her. Then unexpectedly, he stopped, his eyes on the couch. For the longest moment, he didn't say anything. Stephanie held her breath.

"What's all this?"

"Mary and I went shopping."

He made a growling sound in his throat. "I can see that."

She smiled tentatively. "I bought them for you and . . . the house."

His features could've been hacked out of stone. "Take them back!"

"What?"

"I said take them back."

"But . . . why?" Pain slashed her face.

"I don't want them, that's why."

"But . . . you need . . ."

"Dammit, where do you get off telling me what I need?"

The look in his eyes was frightening. Her lower lip trembled. "I didn't mean—"

"I don't care what you meant. Listen up, because I'm not going to say this again." He loomed over her now, his eyes narrowed slits. "I don't need your money or the things it can buy! Understand?"

Stephanie stumbled backward, her eyes rimmed with tears.

"Go on, get out of my sight."

Her lips quivered so hard she could barely get the words out. "I hate you, Flint Carson. I hate . . . you!"

Fourteen

Her soft sobs woke him up.

"Sonofabitch," he hissed, before gritting his teeth and flouncing onto his back.

The sobs continued.

He wouldn't tell her he was sorry because he wasn't, not for sticking up for his rights. But he shouldn't have yelled at her, he decided, staring up at the ceiling. That was childish and immature and totally unlike him to lose control. Usually he was slow to boil. But when he did, he always cut his victim's throat—verbally—with soft, cold, calculated words.

With Stephanie, however, that technique hadn't worked. She made him do crazy things. She made him say crazy things. She made him crazy period.

That was just too damn bad, because if tonight hadn't proved the difference between his life-style and

Stephanie's, then nothing ever would. She was the "haves," and he was the "have nots."

The sobs didn't let up, and a coldness swept over him. He groaned, then pounded the pillow. Damn these cardboard-thin walls, he thought violently. If only she hadn't wanted to remain here...if only he hadn't let her. She hadn't fooled him; he knew what she was up to. She saw him as a challenge. That had to be it. And she wanted him. He saw that, too. Taming this misdirected cowboy was a game, and when she was done, she would cast him aside like a dress she'd worn once and no longer wanted.

So what was the solution? Send her packing. Yeah, first thing in the morning he'd do just that. Meanwhile, he couldn't stand her tears. The sound ripped his gut to shreds.

He untangled his limbs from the sheet, grabbed his jeans and slipped them on. He reached her room seconds later and eased open the door. He got no further. Surprise held him rooted to the spot. She sat in the middle of the bed, the sheet clutched against her, and stared at him through wide, tear-stained eyes.

The night suddenly seemed hot and breathless. Or was it because he couldn't get his breath? The dappled moonlight on her ivory skin was the most beautiful thing he'd ever seen.

His tongue stuck to the roof of his mouth. The realness of the situation rendered the nerves and muscles in his groin tight. But that wasn't all. Instinct told him something momentous was about to happen. He couldn't identify it or understand it, but he felt that whatever it was would change him forever.

"Flint?" Her voice came out a mere whisper.

"I...er...heard you crying."

Her eyes gleamed with fresh tears. "I'm...sorry I disturbed you."

The sheet slipped then, and his breath hung suspended. He knew she was naked. And not just her breasts either. All over. His heart sounded like a gong; he was certain she could hear it. His skin was on fire while his legs trembled as if he'd run uphill.

"Are...are you all right?" he finally managed to get out.

She sniffed. "I'm fine."

Only she wasn't, and they both knew it.

Throwing caution to the wind, he strode to the bed. But when she peered up at him, her lashes clumped together in tiny spikes, he froze again, the visible tension in his body made anything else impossible.

Seconds ticked into a minute, and still their eyes held. The silence grew thicker.

"Flint," she whispered again through slightly parted lips.

That was the break he needed, her husky voice, the quickening pulse at the base of her throat. He knew she was as aroused as he was.

Her words proved him right. "I...don't want you to leave me." Her voice came out as an unsteady thread of sound.

"Are you..."

"Yes, oh yes."

"Stephanie...I..."

As if she sensed he was about to leave, she whispered, "Don't...go. Please."

She became an unwitting conspirator then. Stifling a groan, Flint slowly lifted her to her feet.

"Oh, Flint, I was so...scared." She clutched him hard, then drew back as if unprepared for the hardness that stabbed at her stomach.

"See how much I want you."

Once he shed his jeans, he reached for her again and pulled her cheek onto his chest. His flesh seemed to melt into hers, and he groaned.

"Hold me, hold me," she begged.

Wedged together, they fell back onto the bed. With her pinned beneath him, he simply looked at her. Her hair spilled around her like a swatch of black velvet.

"You're beautiful." His rough tone held reverence.

Silence overtook them. Each wondered if this meshing of their bodies was a mirage, a figment of their imagination. There had been no preplanning, no scheming to experience the ecstasy for the taking. In one moment fear had shackled their bodies—in the next, a burgeoning ache fueled them.

Flint took her mouth, hesitantly at first. But then her warm lips parted and their tongues collided, slippery and coiling. Ignited, he raised his head and gazed at her. Her eyes were closed, her moist lips still parted. Growling deep in his throat, he sank his face in the silk of her hair; he could smell the sun there, and daffodils. He trailed kisses across her shoulders, down her arms, to her hands and felt her flesh quiver.

"You're perfect, every inch of you."

"Oh, Flint," she murmured as he touched several fingers with his tongue before he turned his attention to her breasts. They rose and fell with labored breathing while her nipples pouted and beckoned under his warm mouth.

He continued to lave her nipples, and Stephanie moaned as if goaded by unbridled desire. He shifted positions finally and stapled her flat belly with the same hot nipping kisses, only to then move lower. The instant his tongue touched her with a rhythmlike music, she squirmed and made soft murmuring sounds.

Soon she tried to move away, but he refused to relinquish his prize.

"Please," Stephanie gasped. "You're driving me crazy."

"I know."

She cried out, and he forgot everything but the need to be inside her, to fill her. He began with long and slow strokes, and elevated to quick and hot. She clawed at his back.

Blood thundered through him. "Oh, Stephanie!"

"Now!" she cried.

He wanted to pull back, to prolong the sweet pain, but he couldn't hold off the burning heat that spilled from him. She sucked at the air and cried out again.

Flint held her until their breathing returned to normal. Even at that, an hour passed before he forced out the words that had to be said, past his lips.

"Stephanie."

"Uh-huh?"

"This...doesn't change anything..."

She stiffened against him, then pulled away. "I...know." Her voice was low and broken. "Just please...don't tell me you're sorry."

"Never," he said with rough huskiness, and he reached for her again.

* * *

The following morning, after she had loaded the rental car with the packages she intended to return, Flint intercepted her in the kitchen.

As their eyes met, she couldn't find her breath for the fever his nearness aroused in her.

He averted his gaze and said, "There's something I want you to know."

"What?" she asked, her heart sinking.

"Er...I don't make a habit of making love without—" He broke off, while his Adam's apple convulsed as if something were lodged in his throat.

She couldn't help him out; her own throat was too full.

"Without protection," he got out. "But...last night, I lost control."

"I know."

"So I guess what I'm getting at is it possible..."

"No."

He blinked. "No. Are you sure?"

"It's the wrong time of the month."

He drooped visibly, yet his dark eyes searched her face hungrily.

Unable to stand not touching him, she said, "Look, I've got to go."

Skirting past him, she went out the door.

They acted as if they walked on glass. But that didn't lessen the tension. When they were in the same room, it crackled. One wrong look, one touch, and their emotions would skyrocket again.

She tried to stay away from him as much as she could. She nursed her own hurt and insecurities. So did he.

To relieve her anxieties, Stephanie took long walks and even jogged a few miles. One day Mary came to her rescue, took her to a huge flea market in Canton where she found several pieces of nice jewelry and sent them special delivery to Kathy. It felt good to be back doing her job, which was what she loved best.

Or rather *had* loved best. The instant Flint's mouth had burned a trail down her body, she'd known she would never get him out of her system. But her feelings for him went beyond the physical, though she had to admit she'd never been loved so thoroughly, so deliciously, or so expertly.

Certainly she'd felt nothing like that the few times David had made love to her. And never had he taken the liberties with her body she had allowed Flint. The thoughts of what his mouth and tongue had done to her never failed to bring a scalding flush to her face.

While she basked in his lovemaking, he had touched her on another plane. He had touched her heart. She was in love. For the first time in her life she had fallen in love. So she should deserve to live happily ever after, right? Wrong. Why? Because she had chosen the most pig-headed, stubborn, proud man on the face of the planet, who was not interested in a relationship—long-term or otherwise.

But one thing she knew for certain: she wasn't about to let him push her out of his life before she found the answer.

Today, as she waited for Abe to see her for the final time, that thought was uppermost in her mind.

"Well, young lady, how are you?" Abe asked, suddenly joining Stephanie in one of the small rooms.

She smiled, glad of the interruption. "Fine."

"Well, let's just take a look-see here."

They were quiet while the doctor examined her.

His eyes twinkled. "You're in tip-top shape, my dear."

"Oh, Doctor, that's wonderful news."

"You're free to get on with your life."

If only that were true, she thought with a sinking feeling in the pit of her stomach. Her life would never be the same again. Flint Carson had made sure of that.

Stephanie extended her hand. "I want to thank you for all you've done."

Abe batted the air. "I'm thankful things turned out well for you."

Stephanie smiled again. "I'm sure I'll see you again."

Abe winked. "Count on it."

Later, she was about to get into the car, when an unexpected hand on her arm stopped her. Jerking her head up, she looked into the face of her ex-fiancé.

"David!" she exclaimed. "What on earth?"

The pressure on her arm increased. "Just shut up and get in the car."

"But . . ." she spluttered.

"I said get in the damn car!"

Stephanie did as she was told only because she didn't want to create a scene, something she knew from experience that David was very capable of.

Inside the vehicle Stephanie faced him, and in the coldest voice she could muster said, "What's the meaning of this?"

"Don't play Miss High-and-Mighty with me, sugar. I'm not that dim-witted cowboy."

"What are you doing here, David?" This time her voice sounded tired and bored.

"You know why I'm here."

"How did you find me?" She held up her hand. "No, let me guess. Mother."

He grinned a sly grin. "She still thinks we're a match made in heaven."

"I'll see you in hell first."

He grabbed her wrist. "That may be sooner than you think if you don't give me back my aunt's jewelry."

"I told you that was a done deal," Stephanie retorted, wrenching her arm out of his grip and backing as far against the door as she could.

God, how could she have ever considered marrying him? She shuddered inwardly. Comparing him to Flint—well, there was no comparison. The thought of David touching her ever again made her skin crawl.

David ran a hand through his thinning hair. "Then get them back."

"That's impossible." Deciding to try another tactic, she spread her hands and said, "Look, you know I'm in the business to make money. Now, if I were in the habit of reneging on my sales, I wouldn't be in—"

"I don't give a tinker's damn about your reputation," he snarled. "It's my butt I'm worried about."

"What kind of trouble are you in?" she asked on a resigned sigh.

"Let's just say I owe my bookie more than I can pay."

She gave him an incredulous look. "Oh, David, how could you?"

"Save the platitudes, will you?" He pawed the air. "Those jewels are mine, Stephanie. My aunt promised them to me. And I want them back. I have a buyer who'll pay me probably three times what you sold them for."

"At the risk of sounding like a broken record, it's a done deal."

"Well, I suggest you undo it."

Her chin jutted. "Or what?"

"I'll make you sorry you ever met me."

Without warning, she yanked up the door handle. "Either you get out or I go to the authorities." Seconds ticked by. "It's your choice."

"All right. But I won't give up." He leaned over and trailed his finger down one cheek. "You think on that, sugar, you hear?" Then he got out of the car.

Stephanie managed to control her trembling hands, but it took some doing. He was bluffing, she told herself. Anyway, what could he do? She hadn't lied to him. She no longer had the jewelry. She would put the incident behind her. As long as she kept in mind that he was all talk and no action, she would be fine.

Besides, she wasn't going to let that creep ruin the rest of this beautiful day. Holding that thought, she cranked the car and sped toward the ranch.

And Flint.

Fifteen

Birds chirped busily as they flitted through the tree-tops. A dog barked angrily from the other side of the pond.

"There you go, big fellow," Flint crooned, and with the sun beating down on his back, he brushed the gelding's mane.

The horse nickered, then slapped Flint with his tail.

"Yeah, I know you want me to work on you some more, but no can do. I got a living to make, remember?"

The animal turned solemn eyes on him and stared.

He chuckled. "Okay, okay. One more good brushing, then it's back to the pasture you go."

Flint knew he was wasting time he didn't have. But he couldn't seem to get his gears shifted this morning.

In fact, he hadn't been worth a damn since he'd spent that night in Stephanie's arms.

He would give his blood to make love to her again. The thought of that now made him hard, made him ache. Well, too bad. He'd just have to learn to live with his urges. He was still what he was, and she was still what she was.

Even assuming he was going to make a decent wage on his cattle come market time, he still had zilch to offer her. She was used to the best of everything, while he was content to scrape by on nothing.

His unruly thoughts had numbed him into immobility. The sound of a car door jerked him back into action. He turned around, expecting to see Stephanie. Instead, he saw an unfamiliar woman get out of a Lincoln Town Car and walk toward him.

Instinct told him she was Stephanie's mother. It wasn't so much the resemblance—although the same finely drawn features were obvious—that gave her away. It was the haughty tilt to her nose.

He tossed the brush aside, then pushed back his Stetson and waited. She stopped within arm's reach.

"Are you Flint Carson?" she asked in a perfectly modulated voice.

On closer observation, he noticed that her face was too thin, to the point of gauntness, as was the rest of her body. He could see now where Stephanie got her bent for thinness. But that was where the likeness ended. Stephanie was dark-headed; this woman was blond and not very tall. Even her designer suit failed to hide her bony curves. Yet, she held herself as if she wore the crown jewels fastened beneath the French twist at the nape of her neck.

"Yes ma'am," he said at last in response to her question.

If she caught the mocking edge in his tone, she gave no indication. She clutched her hands tightly in front of her. "Well, I'm Flora Marsh, Stephanie's mother."

Flint could read her mind—she wasn't about to shake his hand for fear of getting something Clorox couldn't take off. He almost laughed aloud.

"Your daughter's not here."

Her nose tilted a little higher. "And just where is she?"

"In town."

"Town?" She looked around. "You mean this godforsaken place has a town?"

"Yes, ma'am," he drawled, a cutting smile on his lips. "And we have indoor toilets, too."

Silence followed as menacing as a jab of a lightning bolt.

Her lips shriveled like a prune. "There's no reason to be crude," she snapped.

"Whatever you say, ma'am."

She flushed, and her eyes blazed, but when she spoke, her voice was cool and composed, "I suppose I should thank you for what you did for my—"

"You don't owe me a thing, lady."

This time she flinched under his savage abruptness. "Well . . . maybe not, but—"

Again he cut her off. "If you'd like to wait for your daughter inside, go ahead. I have work to do."

He meant his rudeness as a slap in the face, and she took it as such. But dammit, if anyone needed to be brought down a notch or two, it was this dame.

"Thank...you," she said in her haughtiest tone yet. "I can assure you that as soon as my daughter gets back, we'll be out of your house."

His only response was to pat the gelding on the butt and watch as the animal swished his tail in response.

"Goodbye, Mr. Carson." Her features were now pale and pinched. "I can assure you that we won't trouble you again."

He tipped his hat. "Yes, ma'am."

When she was out of sight, he thought seriously of jumping in his pickup and heading for the nearest bar and getting blind, stinking drunk. He knew from past experience that wouldn't solve a thing. But manual labor would. He stalked into the barn and grabbed his tools. He discarded his shirt and climbed on the top of the barn that was still intact.

He wasn't stupid or naive enough to believe in love at first sight, Flint reminded himself as he pulverized a two-by-four with a nail and hammer. Nor could it grow and mature unless two people understood and accepted each other. True, he was a man with strong physical hungers, but he did not regard that as the cornerstone of love.

What was perhaps even harder to digest—he thought very carefully about this now—was that once he'd taken Stephanie, she seemed to regard him as more than a bed partner, someone worthy of respect. He silently basked in that newfound pride, thinking that just maybe there was a chance for them.

But with Flora Marsh's untimely arrival, what secret hopes he might have harbored were effectively crushed. The dismal truth again stared him in the face... he had nothing to offer her except himself—and that wasn't good enough.

Flint heard a second car door slam and immediately climbed down from the rafters. Stephanie had returned. She saw him, and just as her mother had, walked toward him. She didn't stop until she was within touching distance.

"What'cha doing?" she asked in her newly developed East Texas twang.

He didn't respond. Their gazes locked, the pointed tip of Stephanie's tongue circled her lips, wetting them.

"Don't," he groaned, thinking about how that hot tongue had dipped into his navel before going lower...

"Flint." Her voice sounded thin, and her color was high, as if she could read his mind.

He ground down on his back jaw. "You've got company."

"Company? Me?"

"Yes."

"Who?"

"Your mother."

Stephanie's face lost its color. "My mother... here?"

"Yep." His tone was mocking. "And she's come to rescue her baby daughter."

The hostile silence stretched while mother and daughter continued to stare at each other.

Finally Flora said, her voice taking on a cajoling, whining tone, "Surely you don't mean you're actually going to stay here?"

"For the final time, yes, I do."

Stephanie turned her back on Flora and walked to the front window. They were in Flint's living room where they had been for the past thirty minutes. Hardly a kind word had passed between them.

When Flint told her that Flora was here, she was stunned. First David, then her mother. She'd decided she had definitely done something wrong to deserve such punishment.

Flora's unexpected appearance shouldn't have been a surprise. But somehow it was. She hadn't thought her mother cared enough to see firsthand that her only child was all right. But then, Stephanie suspected that wasn't the reason Flora came, although she never got a straight answer out of her.

"Well, I simply won't leave without you, that's all," Flora said to Stephanie's back. "I just can't stand the thought of you being in these woods another minute . . . or with that . . . distasteful man."

Stephanie swung around. Her eyes flashed. "God, Mother, you're something else. You didn't even know 'that man' until a few minutes ago. So how can you judge him?"

"Oh, I can judge him all right," Flora replied haughtily, moving to the edge of the couch. "I know all about him. When you told me where you were, I had him checked out."

Stephanie gasped. "You never cease to amaze me."

"Now, darling, don't take that attitude. I did it for your own good."

"I suppose that's why you told David where I was." Stephanie's voice was rich in sarcasm.

"Exactly. You've hurt him badly, and I think you should reconsider. After all, he's our kind—"

"Spare me, Mother. I'm sure you don't know this about your sanctimonious David." Something hard crept into Stephanie's eyes. "But he's so desperate for money to pay off his bookie that he's threatening me because I won't return his aunt's jewelry to him."

Flora raised a hand to her chest. "Oh dear, how awful. Threatening you? I had no idea."

"Oh, really."

Flora colored. "Well, maybe he isn't right for you. But then neither is that—" she broke off, distaste lowering her voice "—drunken, has-been cop."

"Stop! Stop right now!" Stephanie's voice gained strength. "You have no right to say that about him!"

Flora's lips tightened. "The fact that I'm your mother gives me that right. And I know he's not for you. And I don't want you getting involved with the likes of him. It isn't only a question of different backgrounds, Steph."

Her tone grew suddenly warmer. "It goes much deeper than that. Surely you haven't turned a blind eye on how hard, how crudely he lives." A shudder shook her frame. "How you've stayed here as long as you have is beyond me."

"Are you finished now, Mother?" Stephanie demanded coldly.

"Only if you'll admit that it'll take a woman of his own kind who can make him happy."

"You can stop worrying," Stephanie said, scraping over the pain. "Even if I wanted him, he doesn't want me."

"Thank God one of you has some sense."

Stephanie swallowed around the lump in her throat. "Yeah."

"So you are coming with me?" Flora asked, her tone brighter, as if sensing she had won the battle if not the war.

"No. I'll leave in my own good time and not a minute before."

Realizing she had pushed as far as she dared, Flora stood, then crossed to Stephanie. The kiss, when it came, was as cool as her mother's lips. Stephanie forced herself not to flinch.

"I'll expect a call the second you get back to your apartment. We'll have lunch and put this unfortunate episode behind us."

"Take care, Mother," Stephanie said in a flat voice.

Once the Lincoln was nothing but a cloud of dust, Stephanie walked back to the barn. The door to the storeroom was open. Through it, she could see Flint.

"Hi," she said tentatively, standing in the doorway.

He turned slowly, and her heart stumbled. He looked as hard as a statue and just as unyielding.

"It won't work," she said quickly.

His eyes were vacant. "I don't know what you're talking about."

"Yes you do. You're trying to shut me out. Again." She ignored his smirk and went on, "I think we should talk."

"So talk."

"We . . . we have to come to terms with what . . . happened between us."

"There's nothing to come to terms with." He scowled.

"I don't believe that, and neither do you."

A vein jumped in his temple. "Where's your mother?"

"Gone."

"I expected you to go with her. She said you didn't belong here, right?"

"Yes, but it doesn't matter what she said. I'm a big girl now. My mother no longer controls my life."

"Sure."

Stephanie gave him a measured look. "I can understand why you'd think differently with her coming on like gangbusters." His smirk was more pronounced this time. "And that's what she did, right?"

"She's a hard woman."

"And one who doesn't know how to love," Stephanie whispered softly. "It's a frightening thing to realize that about your own mother, but I finally did. And when it happened, it set me free."

It was the first time she had admitted out loud the emptiness she had felt as the only child of the autocratic Flora Marsh. Flora had mastered the ability to take from others without giving anything of herself in return. At one time Stephanie had admired that trait. Now it sickened her.

"So back to us," she whispered into the silence.

"Look, just because you're no longer influenced by your mother doesn't change things."

"Yes, it does." A sense of futility filled Stephanie, but she fought against it. "Don't you see—"

"Save it," he spat. "Your mother's right. You don't belong here."

His words were like a hot poker. "Is that Flora talking or you?"

"Me."

The silence in the room suddenly turned into a wall of ice.

"I don't know if you're just too shortsighted," Stephanie said, shaking inside, "or just too pigheaded to see what's right in front of your face!"

With that she turned and flounced to the door.

"Stephanie?"

She eased around, her heart lodged in her throat, hope burning in her eyes. "Yes?"

He opened his mouth, only to close it suddenly. "Forget it."

Pain swept through her. She wrapped her arms around herself and kicked the door closed with a bang.

Sixteen

Two weeks. Such a short time for so much to have happened. A frown slipped across Stephanie's face. Before the crash, life had been relatively simple. Now everything had shifted; she had to cope with a new world. She wondered if her life would ever be the same again. No. Flint had seen to that.

How could she have known that it would be this moody, withdrawn rancher who would steal her heart? But something special had drawn them together, and she had willfully turned her back on the past to follow the overpowering promptings of her heart.

And as foolish as that was, Stephanie was determined to go for the heretofore elusive mother lode—a declaration of love from Flint and subsequent commitment.

With each day that passed, it became more difficult to hide her feelings. She ached to feel his arms around her again, ached to confess her love.

Fear kept her mute. She knew he wanted her, but lust was not the same as love. Time was running out. She couldn't remain where she wasn't wanted much longer.

While this thought weighed on her, Stephanie trudged outside to the swing on the front porch. Instead of sitting down, she walked to the edge of the house and gazed toward the far pasture. Flint and Smitty, barely visible, toiled over another rotting string of fences.

Stephanie had hoped Flint wouldn't work until dark. It looked as if she wasn't going to get her wish. She'd gone to the grocery store earlier and had plans for them to share dinner.

Since her mother's unexpected visit two days ago, she'd only had glimpses of him. He'd planned it that way, she knew. The strain of being under the same roof and not touching told on both of them.

When the two men showed no signs of quitting, she turned away, her shoulders slightly slumped. That was when she saw him. Rage flooded through her. And fear.

David Weston got out of his car, his narrowed eyes targeted on her.

"What are you doing here?" she hissed.

His gait brought him within a hair's breadth of her. "I warned you, remember?"

"You're drunk!" Disgusted, she stepped back.

He grabbed her wrist. "Oh, no, you don't."

"Take your hands off me!"

His hold on her tightened. "No way, baby. Either you give me the money, or I'm going to do something we'll both be sorry for." He slammed her against the side of the house and dug his fingernails into her skin.

At first she hadn't thought he could possibly harm her. She wasn't so sure anymore. She sensed he would derive great pleasure in taking his anger and frustrations out on her. He was demented.

"So what's it going to be?"

His foul breath sprayed her face. She tried to turn away, but he grabbed her chin and held her steady. "Flint will kill you."

"But lover boy's not here." His hands squeezed her shoulders. "It's just you and me, baby."

Lobbing her head to one side, Stephanie struggled for enough breath to try to reason with him. "Please...don't hurt me."

Flint blinked the sweat out of his eyes and glanced at his watch. "Let's call it a day, Smitty."

"Okay by me, boss." Sweating as profusely as Flint, Smitty mopped his handlebar mustache with a rag. "I'm bushed."

"Me too. This heat is something else."

Smitty grimaced. "Thought this was spring."

"Yeah, me, too."

They fell silent as they made ready to leave, so tired they could hardly walk. Yet Flint was reluctant to go home.

What to do about Stephanie gnawed at him constantly. He tried to close his thoughts to her.

At the memory of her naked body first touching his, he experienced again the electrifying shock that had gone through him. Then every other aspect of that night flowed hotly as well. In swelling discomfort, he swung onto the back of the gelding.

Smitty mounted his horse, and together they rode toward the house. Flint saw them before they saw him. He pulled up short, and though his face showed no emotion at all, his blood turned to ice water.

"Something wrong, boss?"

"Yeah. Follow me." Flint nudged his animal into a full gallop.

A minute later they rode into the yard. Flint saw Stephanie pinned against the house by that insensitive scumbag. Worse still, Flint knew Weston was aware that riders were approaching, but he didn't release his hold on Stephanie. It seemed as if he was so pumped up, so hellbent on his mission that nothing or no one could stop him.

Primitive rage boiled through Flint. He would have liked nothing better than to beat David Weston to within an inch of his life.

Instead he remained in the saddle and said, "Let her go, Weston."

Breathing heavily, David dropped his hands, turned and glared at Flint. Flint wasn't looking at him; his eyes were on Stephanie.

"Did he hurt you?"

Stephanie drew a deep, shuddering breath and shook her head. "No."

"Now you listen here, Carson, my quarrel isn't with you."

While slowly climbing off his horse, Flint's gaze reverted back to Weston.

"She's got something that belongs to me, and I aim to—"

"Shut up," Flint said softly.

If he had reached out and hit David, the effect could not have been more alarming. David's eyes widened, and his jaw dropped. As he tried to speak, his Adam's apple twitched convulsively in his neck.

"I'm telling you—"

"Only I'm not listening," Flint said in an unruffled voice. He walked toward David with an easy, uncoiling motion. He looked him full in the face, his eyes as cold as metal. "You go on now. Get off my property."

No one said a word. No one moved. Even the air was still.

Finally Flint turned to his ranch hand. "Ah, hell, Smitty, on second thought, call the sheriff. Tell him to come pick up this piece of garbage."

"No...please," David whimpered, and stumbled backward toward his vehicle. "I won't bother her again." His narrow shoulders bent under the burden of humiliation.

"Go on, get the hell outta my sight."

Minutes later, Flint and Stephanie were alone. Stephanie peered at him, her heart reflected in her eyes.

"Don't...don't look at me like that." His voice held torment.

"What next, Flint?" she whispered.

"I...er...just wanted to make sure you were all right."

Flint hadn't been able to stay away from her. After the confrontation with David, Stephanie had showered, then disappeared inside her room where she had remained. She'd told him she wanted to be alone.

As tired as he was, sleep should have been no problem, only it was. It eluded him. So to quiet the beast raging inside him, he'd gone to check on her, to see for himself that she was indeed all right.

She had responded to his knock with a soft "Come in." Now, standing poised in the middle of the room, she stared at him with unwavering eyes. "I'm fine." Her lower lip, however, made a liar out of her; it trembled.

Flint needed no other motivation. He closed the distance between them and swooped her up in his arms.

"Flint?"

Ignoring the husky question, he crossed the room and deposited her on the bed. Whether from exertion or from rising passion, his voice came out a growl. "A little while ago you asked what was next. This is my answer."

He straightened, and with jerky movements stripped off his clothes, then sat back down beside her. Their heads came together, and the consuming hotness of his mouth closed over hers. His hands peeled off her clothing.

They drifted back on the bed and breathlessly played with each other, touching and stroking, and kissing, his lips never far from her flesh.

He pulled his mouth away and said thickly, "Not yet."

She held onto him, a trembling shape in the darkness as he sank his lips onto her breasts with such fierce intensity that it seemed to pull at all her nerve endings.

"Please..." she urged, gripping his buttocks.

He raised himself over her, moved his pelvis, then entered her. A moan slipped past her lips, and she twisted her hands around the small of his back and arched against him, pushing his full length inside her until there was nowhere left to go.

"Oh, Flint," she said tremulously, kissing his neck with her open lips and darting tongue. "You...you just seem to consume me."

His answering whisper breathed past her ear. "Don't talk, just feel."

To Flint, feeling that soft warmth yield to his bold hardness was a miracle—an ecstasy of awareness that forever increased his pleasure even as it increased his determination to clutch at the intangible something hidden beyond the wall of her giving flesh.

He told himself that it was enough merely to be inside her, but it wasn't enough. He knew it, just as he knew that despite her participation in the act, she, too, sought something beyond the act itself.

"Oh, yes," Stephanie cried, clinging to him, while urgency changed to blind panic as their bodies danced to a climax that endured endlessly, then slowly eased. And they emerged, dazed and spent, but with each heart beating its own endless message.

Before dawn she took him, her lips sliding the length of him, defining him. She wanted desperately for this night never to end, even as he made a guttural sound and reached for her. Then she was flipped into the air so that she was atop him.

From there she rained kisses over his chest, his nipples, while he lifted her effortlessly up and she at last felt him hard inside her. She gasped, but then felt him fill her with such ease that a warmth seeped through her that was only partially sexual, a warmth that encompassed a great deal more.

Time moved unhurried, seeming to pause only at intervals, as if listening for the excited moans, the meaningless murmurs that carried them into the morning's early glow.

"I don't think I could've lasted much longer without this," he murmured when they were spent once again.

"Me neither," she said.

They were quiet for a moment, then Stephanie caressed the ugly scar on his side.

"Nasty, isn't it?"

"Does it hurt?" Stephanie asked, her gaze troubled.

"Not anymore."

"Do you think you'll ever go back?"

"I don't want to."

"Then don't."

He moved out of her arms and stacked his hands behind his head. "It's not that simple. My herd has to bring in some money."

"It will. It just has to. I can't stand the thought of you going back to that horrible job."

"If I had listened to my gut instinct, it might not have ended the way it did."

"You mean the bust."

"Yeah, the bust that went sour."

"Surely they don't blame you."

"No, but I blame myself." Flint paused and breathed deeply. "There was a snitch inside, and I didn't know it."

"Then how could you blame yourself?"

"I knew something was rotten in Denmark, but I didn't listen to instincts."

"Did they finally catch them?"

"Finally."

"It was afterward that...your wife left you, wasn't it?"

Although she felt him stiffen, he eventually answered her. "That's right."

"What happened?"

"We were on a collision course from the beginning, I just didn't see it." Regret, rather than pain, roughened his tone. "She wanted 'things' while I wanted kids. So we decided to compromise and wait." He paused.

"Go on," she encouraged, rubbing her hand over his hard, flat belly.

"Then I killed my first person. She couldn't take it. And I was drinking heavily. But the end came when she decided I couldn't keep her in the style to which she was accustomed, so she told me to take a hike. End of story."

Stephanie fought back the tears. "Not every woman is like her, you know?"

He didn't say anything.

"I love you, Flint." There, she'd said it. She had bared her soul to this hard man, and even if he trampled it, she couldn't have not said those words.

"Don't say that . . ." he said brokenly.

"I know you don't love me . . ."

He was so long in responding again that she feared he wasn't going to. Her heart ached.

"But I do love you," he whispered, "only—"

Untold joy swept through her, but the qualifier on the end was a threat to be reckoned with.

"I can make you happy, Flint."

He didn't answer, and she feared he was retreating to his dark thoughts, shutting her out. Determined not to let that happen, she trailed a finger down the side of his face and smiled. "I can also be happy living here."

"You say that now . . ."

"I'll prove it to you," she said fiercely. "You just wait and see."

Flint's eyes shone as they melted into hers. And then, in response to a signal that struck silently but unerringly, they dived back into each other's arms.

Gone was the probing into a bleak and chilling past. Nothing but their revived need of each other was of importance. He crushed her against him with a pressure born of desperation, and his mouth was over hers like an open furnace. An answering fire flamed within her.

Beyond all restraint, their bodies became one.

Seventeen

An early moon rose above the pines. Flint paused atop his horse and looked as far as the eye could see. Instead of going home, after leaving Ed's house, he'd saddled his gelding and ridden off into the sunset.

His analogy drew a smirk across his lips. John Wayne might have ridden into that proverbial sunset, all right, but he couldn't. Usually, though, an outing such as this calmed the restlessness inside him. Not today.

When he'd brought Stephanie to the ranch, he had had no name for what he sought so feverishly. And with each possession of her body that elusive "something" had returned to taunt him.

When he'd finally put a name to it, he'd been stunned. He'd wanted more than her fiery responses to his body; he'd wanted her to love him.

And now that he had her love, he didn't know what to do with it. Pain lashed through him so intensely it almost took his breath away. He couldn't ask her to marry him. That was out of the question. She didn't belong here no matter what she said. Could he let her go?

He didn't know. He honestly didn't know.

The house was empty without Flint.

Stephanie had spent the better part of the day with Mary. They had visited a friend of Mary's who wanted to sell a bracelet filled with twenty silver heart charms from the 1930s. She had leapt at the chance to buy it and was still extremely excited over her good fortune.

Even now, as she lay on the couch and waited for Flint to come home, she eyed the bracelet. She couldn't wait to call Kathy. For the moment, though, her thoughts were on Flint. Something had to give. She could not continue the emotional tug-of-war with him any longer. She ached to know what the future held for them, or if they even *had* a future.

When they had confessed their love to each other a week ago, Stephanie had hoped they could begin to work toward a future together. She'd known it wouldn't be easy, that it would be a battle, but with love the motivator, anything was possible.

There were times when he lowered that cold facade and allowed her to see another Flint, a lighthearted, talkative one. He was a different person from the surly stranger who had so coldly rebuffed her that day on the plane.

Yesterday's incident jumped to mind, and she found herself smiling. He had insisted she learn to ride a horse. Although she had protested, he'd been adamant. After several unsuccessful attempts, she had finally mastered the technique of handling the gentle mare.

She and Flint had been touring the pasture and had stopped at the pond for the horses to drink when the incident happened. Flint had already dismounted and led his gelding to the nearest tree and was watching her under the brim of his hat. "I think Henrietta has had enough to drink," he had drawled.

Stephanie had turned, flashed him a smile, then patted the mare on the side. "No, she hasn't. Can't you see how thirsty she is?"

"Doesn't matter. It's not a good idea to let 'em drink too much too fast."

"Oh, all right," Stephanie said, pulling on the reins. "But it sounds like cruel and unusual punishment to me."

He harrumphed. "It's cruel and unusual punishment if you don't—"

"Oh, my God!" Her terrified scream cut off his sentence. "What's she doing! What's happening!"

The horse had paid no attention to her hard jerk on the reins and was wading deeper into the water.

"No! Stop!" she cried, yanking even harder on the leather straps.

Stephanie's panicked cry went unheeded. Flint reached the bank just as the horse rolled over and unceremoniously dumped her in the water.

"Oh!" she wailed, feeling her tennis shoes sink into the mud. She struggled to maintain her footing.

Flint stood with his arms crossed and peered down at her. "Mmm, nice day for a swim," he said, a grin tacked on his face.

"Why...you...you...!"

"Tut, tut." His grin broadened. "Don't say it. Don't even think it."

"But...but," Stephanie spluttered, placing her hands on her hips and aching to slap that smug grin off his face.

Flint threw back his head and laughed.

"Don't you dare laugh at me, you big bully."

"If you could only see yourself."

"I don't want to see myself! I know I look a horrible mess, thanks to you and that...that horse..." She gave Henrietta a scathing glare. "Why'd she do that to me, anyway?" she asked, extending her hand to Flint so he could pull her out. "I never did anything to her."

He laughed again. "Ah, don't take offense. That's just her way of telling you how much she likes you."

"Sure." She cut another glance at the mare and muttered. "You big dummy."

Flint's warm chuckle drew her back to him. His eyes moved over her, made her conscious that her wet T-shirt clearly outlined her full breasts and distended nipples.

A scorching heat flooded through her.

He cleared his throat. "Speaking of lying down."

"Here?" Her limbs felt suddenly boneless.

"Why not?"

Stephanie looked around and noticed how secluded they were. "No...reason."

He grinned and reached for her. "I kinda thought you'd see it my way..."

While there had been other tender moments, there had also been other dark ones. The old wall would suddenly appear, and he'd shut her out. Except physically. Flint's appetite for her was insatiable, as hers was for him. The nights found them linked passionately, exploring each other anew, with only the briefest of respites.

But that wasn't enough. She wanted more. She wanted a full commitment and would not settle for less.

The sudden jangle of the phone shattered her thoughts, which was just as well, she told herself.

"Oh, hi, Kat," she said after a moment. "I was just going to call you." She eased down on the couch. "You'll never guess what I found today..."

She was in the middle of describing the treasure when she felt an odd sensation climb her spine. Clutching the receiver, she spun around. Flint stood in the doorway, an odd expression on his face.

"Kat, look, I'll call you back in a minute, okay?"

Once the call was terminated, she stood and gave Flint a wobbly smile. "You're home," she said inanely.

"You miss your work, don't you?"

"Of course I do, but—"

"Then maybe you ought to go back."

A sudden tension gripped her. "We're not talking about my job here, are we?"

"No." The reply came in a strained growl.

"So what are you saying, Flint?" Was he telling her to go? No! She wasn't ready for that.

"Stephanie..." Flint shook his head, his thoughts taking trails she could not follow.

Helplessness threatened to destroy her composure. She had only one recourse and that was to say the only thing that had any meaning in this endless moment of pain.

"I love you, Flint," she whispered brokenly. "You know that, don't you?"

He stared gravely at her for a long moment, then let his hard-held breath out like a sigh. "Yes," he said. "I'm afraid I do."

"Don't be afraid, my darling. I'm not."

He turned away in slow degrees, as if he couldn't bear to look into her eyes.

"You...told me you loved me," she said, squeezing the words out.

He twisted back around, and she watched as that closed look wiped all expression from his face.

"What is it you want from me?" he asked.

"I have to know where I stand with you," she cried in a low voice. "I have to know what you're prepared to give."

"That's just it," he said tonelessly. "I have nothing to give."

"You have yourself."

"And you deserve better. Don't you understand, I can't give you what you're used to, what you need."

"I don't want things, I want you."

"You say that now, but what about later?"

Stephanie hardly breathed. "For God's sake, my love for you isn't some passing fancy."

"What happens if I decide ranching isn't for me? Or better yet, what if I can't make a go of this place?

Then what?'' His eyes flared in his weathered face. ''Well, I'll tell you what. I'll have to go back to the agency, and I wouldn't ask another woman to go through that again.''

''Are you . . . going back to the agency?''

''I don't know.''

''Well, we'll just have to cross that bridge when we come to it.''

He shoved blunt fingernails through his hair. ''It's not that simple.''

''I'm not like your ex-wife, Flint,'' she said in a soft choked voice.

''You think I don't know that?'' His voice sounded warped. ''Oh, hell, maybe we should discuss this tomorrow.''

Stephanie turned her back on him, feeling sick. That something special between them had disappeared and had left only a room full of emptiness. She had never felt so unwanted and useless.

''There won't be a tomorrow, Flint.'' Her voice faded until it eased altogether. But she wouldn't cry. She wouldn't give him the satisfaction. Still, it was an effort to speak again. ''You're right, there's nothing here for me.''

''There never was. I tried to tell you that, only you wouldn't listen.''

The silence of the room became a cold and alien thing that clamped down around them and held them helpless.

Tragedy had thrown them together. Desire had kept them together. Now harsh pride was parting them.

Stephanie put a hand to her throat. In that soundless void, her voice, when it finally came, sounded raw and loud. ''Not only are you a fool, Flint Carson, but you're a coward. A damned coward!''

"Stephanie…" Her name came out an agonized cry. She left without another word.

Eighteen

"**Y**ou won't believe it!"

Stephanie turned from the filing cabinet and stared at Kathy Gentry. "Won't believe what?"

They were in Stephanie's cubbyhole of an office. She had been trying to get some much-needed book work done, but as usual she found it hard to concentrate.

"Get this. Mrs. Hoffman bought that Battenbury tablecloth and matching napkins." The scattering of freckles across Kathy's nose stood out, calling attention to her pert features. "Yeah, that old tightwad finally coughed up some real cash."

Stephanie's lips twitched. "You shouldn't talk about Mrs. Hoffman like that."

"Why?" Kathy quipped with a grin. "It's the truth, and *you* know it."

A smile lit Stephanie's entire face. "Did she really pay cash?"

"As in the cold, hard kind." Kathy paused and cocked her head slightly. "You know that's the first time I've seen you really smile in two months."

Stephanie sighed. "I'm sorry I've been such a pain in the butt."

"Hey, you don't owe me an apology. I know you're going through a private hell right now. I just wish there was something I could do to help."

"You have. You've kept the store afloat, and you've been my friend." Stephanie had confided in Kathy up to a point about Flint and their relationship simply because she hadn't been able to keep it bottled inside her.

"I've loved doing both."

Stephanie took a deep breath and changed the subject. "Don't I have something I'm supposed to do this afternoon?"

"Yep. A meeting with a pawnshop dealer in Lufkin about that garnet necklace."

Stephanie snapped her fingers. "That's right. And I should be leaving shortly, too."

They discussed several other items of business, then Kathy left. Stephanie stared at her desk, thinking she ought to straighten it. But she didn't; she walked to the window and stared outside. Instead of seeing the tall buildings that lined the city streets, she saw tall trees, a pasture strewn with wildflowers and cattle. And in the midst of that, she saw a horse and rider.

In an effortless gesture, she summoned Flint before her. His face was so vivid in its nearness that she clearly saw the thick-lashed eyes, the sensual lips framing words she couldn't understand. Suddenly she was seized by an inexplicable panic.

Would she ever fill the void in her life that losing him had created? She closed her eyes and felt the ever-present sadness gnaw at her. After returning to her apartment in Houston, she had been both furious and heartbroken. But it was the former that had given her the grit to finally say to hell with him. If he didn't want her, she didn't want him.

Too, there had been the niggling at the back of her mind that maybe there was truth in what he had said. Maybe she did belong to the city, among the bright lights, the parties, the loud and boisterous friends.

Only they were both wrong. Dead wrong. When she couldn't function after dreaming of him every night— of his hungry kisses, of his groans as he took her, sometimes tender, sometimes savage, the laughter when it came—she knew she no longer belonged here. She belonged with him. She belonged *to* him. And without him, her life was an empty shell.

Yet through all the pain and despair, she had harbored hope that he would come to his senses, see what he was throwing away with so little thought. But when the hours stretched into days and the days into months, that hope vanished.

Around her friends, which included Mary Liscomb, who had visited her twice, her customers and her mother, she put on a brave front. But she hadn't fooled anyone. Even Flora had tempered her tone and seemed genuinely worried about her.

And with good reason, because she never slowed down. Work was her panacea for coping, for getting up each morning. And though Collections by

Stephanie's bank account reflected this hard work, it had taken its toll. Her bones ached. Her appetite diminished. And the loneliness was poison inside her.

Still, she'd known then, just as she knew now, that she had done the right thing. Unless he could return her love, she was better off without him. And soon he wouldn't mean any more to her than a stranger on the street.

But not today.

"Stephanie."

Startled, she spun around.

"Sorry," Kathy said, "but you told me not to let you forget your appointment."

"Thanks. I'm on my way."

A few minutes later, purse in hand, she forced her shoulders back and walked into the waning sunlight.

For two weeks Flint stayed close to the ranch, though he spent more hours brooding than he did working. He took care of his cattle because he had to, and when he could choke it down, he ate a little food.

He turned into a mere caricature of his former self. Weight fell off him. His eyes became listless, sunken caves carving his cheekbones deeper, and his skin had lost much of its tan.

Where once he'd moved with catlike agility, he now trudged heavy-footed.

"How much longer do you intend to keep this up?"

Flint didn't so much as flinch at the sound of Ed's voice, nor did he bother to look up. Instead, he swung the ax until the piece of pine looked like chop suey. "As long as it takes, I reckon."

"Care to talk?"

"Nope." Flint paused and wiped his face across his sleeve. "Just got an itch I can't scratch, that's all."

Ed rested his arms across his pot belly. "I guess that's one way of puttin' it. But we both know what that itch is, don't we?"

"Ed, I'm not in the mood for this small talk crap."

"So I won't make small talk. I'll hit you with the big stuff. You're a fool."

Flint laughed without humor. "Tell me something I don't know."

A long, heavy silence followed.

At last Ed said, "Mary's seen her twice."

Flint's jaws tightened. He went right on with his chore.

Ed watched him a moment longer, then with a disgusted shake of his head, he turned and stamped off.

"How . . . how is she?"

Ed halted, then eased back around. "She loves you just as you are, you know, only you're too damned dim-witted to see that."

Not bothering to wait for a reply, Ed turned again and ambled off, leaving Flint staring at him with his mouth gaping open.

Bone weary, Flint made his way toward the house. But when he reached the back door, he froze.

He couldn't do it. He couldn't walk across that threshold again and face the emptiness inside. He looked toward the sun quickly, seeking it's warmth for his chilled body. But on the other side of that door there was no sunlight to relieve the darkness inside his soul or blot out the loneliness that touched every nerve in his body and held him captive.

Stephanie was everywhere—her face, her smell, her laughter—on the back of his eyelids, in his cup of coffee and in every room in the house.

Turning, he stumbled down the steps and over to the nearest tree. He faced the sun once again, while tears streamed down his cheeks.

What was he going to do? How was he going to keep living without her? Had Ed leveled with him? Did she love him for what he was, not for what he should be? Dare he hope? Dare he take the chance? In that instant the decision came. He knew not how or why. He knew only he couldn't exist another day without her.

He had to try to right a terrible wrong. He had to bring her back. Then he had to prove that he wasn't the coward she thought he was, that having her beside him, if only for one day, was better than not having her at all.

But all of the above entailed work and a sacrifice of further patience. He had to fix up the house, make it worthy of her. He had to finish the barn, manicure the lawns and pastures beyond, and sell his herd . . .

A tall order, but he could do it. *He would do it.*

He secured his Stetson on his head, turned on his heels and strode toward the barn. For the first time in a long while, there was a confident swagger to Flint's step.

Flint didn't know how long he'd sat in the pickup before he mustered enough nerve to get out and walk to the front door.

Still he hesitated. It had been four months since he'd sent Stephanie away. What if he'd waited too long? What if she'd stopped loving him?

What was at stake with this visit sent the blood rushing to his head. God, but it ached, as though two boxers were slugging it out inside. Nor could he seem to get a decent breath and keep it.

When he reached the front door and touched the brass knob, he noticed his hand shook. His newfound courage began to slip. He dug deep for another breath, ignoring his heart tripping like a jackhammer, and his legs trembled as though he'd run the few yards instead of walking.

He rubbed his thigh with a sweaty palm, then knocked on the door. No response. He knocked harder and longer. Still no answer. He poised his fist to strike again when the door opened. The next instant he was face-to-face with Stephanie.

"For crying out loud...you don't," she began hotly, only to end in a faltering whisper, "knock...the door down," and stood there, her face chalk white.

The silence that enveloped them was so complete, it was deafening. Flint used the opportunity to drink in the sight of her. Though more slender than he remembered, and the bruised circles under her eyes more pronounced, she was still as lovely as ever.

At last, and into the oppressive stillness, he dropped his voice, but it seemed very far away. "Hello, Stephanie."

Her lips scarcely moved. "Good...evening."

The frigid formality in her tone locked his throat against further speech. Flint shifted positions, then cleared his throat, the sound harsh and raw in his ears. "Aren't you going to ask me in?"

"Why should I?"

He stood there, dying on the inside. His worst fears had come to pass and he had lost. She behaved like a statue carved out of ice. Those enormous blue eyes held no warmth. They were fixed on him with such contempt that Flint felt a corrosive acid burn his insides.

Desperate to free himself from the paralysis crippling him, he forced words around the constriction in his throat, only to discover his superhuman effort had produced only a rasping whisper.

"The reason I know is because..." he began, and felt his throat close completely.

"Go on."

Stephanie's voice was clear and utterly detached. She wasn't going to make it easy.

"...I love you and want to marry you," he said in another raspy whisper.

"What?" Her lips moved stiffly.

He stepped closer, but still he didn't touch her. "Oh, God, Steph, can you forgive me for being such a fool?"

Her composure crumpled, and two big tears trickled down her face. "Oh, Flint."

Matching tears rolled down his cheeks. "I'll make it up to you, I promise."

"Will you just shut up, you big jerk." And having said that, she cried, "Oh, Flint! Please hold me. I won't believe this until you do!"

She need not have asked. He was already reaching for her.

Rain fell.

Flint dreamed of Stephanie; her flesh was moist and cool, as if it had been rained on.

He felt movement beside him suddenly, and his eyes opened. He hadn't been dreaming. The flesh-and-blood Stephanie was beside him, her long, smooth limbs tangled with his hard-muscled ones. His heart leapt, and he smiled. And remembered.

For the first time ever, he felt good inside, free of pain, whole. *Love could do that,* she had whispered a while ago when she was on top, with him rising strong and gloved in her warmth.

"Flint..."

He shifted so that he could gaze down at her. "Mmm?"

"Hi," she whispered, moving closer to him.

His flesh trembled. "Hi, yourself."

"What are you thinking?"

"About how much I love you and how close I came to losing you."

"You know that I never worried about your lack of 'things.'"

"I do now. So will you marry me?"

"When?"

He chuckled. "God, woman, you're easy."

"What can I say?" Stephanie quipped saucily. "I think it'd be nice to get married at Ed and Mary's."

"That is a good idea." His eyes turned serious. "By the way, I have a surprise for you."

"I hate surprises."

"Naw, all women love surprises."

She nipped him on the shoulder. "So tell me."

"See there, you can't stand it." Flint tweaked her on the nose before going on, "I remodeled the house and finished the barn."

She scooted up, cradled her head in her hand and peered down at him. "You did? But...how...so quickly?"

"Ed and Mary and Smitty." He grinned. "I've been such a tight ass, they were all about ready to ship me off with the next load of cattle."

She kissed his shoulder this time, and he groaned. "Missed me, huh?"

"More than you'll ever know."

"Me, too."

"What about your mother?"

Stephanie grew pensive for a moment. "I hope in time she'll come around." She broke off with a grin. "Actually I'm counting on your charm to win her over."

He made a growling noise in his throat, then answered her grin with one of his own. "I'll give it my best shot, but I'm making no promises. Your mother is something else."

"I know." She was quiet for a moment. "What...about the agency?"

"I'm not going back."

Her relief was obvious. "Have you told Lee?"

"Nope, but I'm going to when I invite him to the wedding."

"Regardless of what you decided, I would've supported you."

"Thank you for saying that." His voice was thick.

She drummed her fingers softly against his thighs.

"I can't think when you do that."

"I know," she said weakly.

Flint swallowed and forced himself to say what was in his heart. "Even though my cattle's in great de-

mand, we won't be rich, but we won't starve, either."
His eyes held a sober question mark.

"Course we won't, silly. I plan to work, too. I've
been thinking about opening up a small store in
Crockett."

"What about Houston?"

"Kathy thinks she can scrape together the funds to
buy me out."

"Whatever it takes to make you happy, I'm all for
it."

"Oh, Flint, I love you," she said with soft sweetness.

"And I love you."

"Kiss me." Her tone held sudden urgency.
"Please."

Her eyes fluttered closed as his open mouth came
down over hers. On fire, she moved her fingers down
the rigid contours of his back while he shifted her hips
back into steamy contact with his groin.

"I love you," she muttered breathlessly.

"I'll make you happy."

Their tongues flickered and met. There was an ex-
quisite pain inside Flint as she circled her buttocks
against him. "You already have, my darling," he
ground out thickly.

When they were able to talk again, he whispered,
"Are you ready to go home?"

Stephanie's features were suddenly wreathed in a
radiant smile. "I thought you'd never ask."

* * * * *

Bestselling author **NORA ROBERTS** captures all the romance, adventure, passion and excitement of Silhouette in a special miniseries.

THE
CALHOUN WOMEN

Four charming, beautiful and fiercely independent sisters set out on a search for a missing family heirloom—an emerald necklace—and each finds something even more precious...passionate romance.

Look for THE CALHOUN WOMEN miniseries starting in June.

COURTING CATHERINE
in Silhouette Romance #801 (June/$2.50)

A MAN FOR AMANDA
in Silhouette Desire #649 (July/$2.75)

FOR THE LOVE OF LILAH
in Silhouette Special Edition #685 (August/$3.25)

SUZANNA'S SURRENDER
in Silhouette Intimate Moments #397 (September/$3.29)

SILHOUETTE·INTIMATE·MOMENTS®

IT'S TIME TO MEET
THE MARSHALLS!

In 1986, bestselling author Kristin James wrote A VERY SPECIAL FAVOR for the Silhouette Intimate Moments line. Hero Adam Marshall quickly became a reader favorite, and ever since then, readers have been asking for the stories of his two brothers, Tag and James. At last your prayers have been answered!

In August, look for THE LETTER OF THE LAW (IM #393), James Marshall's story. If you missed youngest brother Tag's story, SALT OF THE EARTH (IM #385), you can order it by following the directions below. And, as our very special favor to you, we'll be reprinting A VERY SPECIAL FAVOR this September. Look for it in special displays wherever you buy books.

Available now at your favorite retail outlet, or order your copy by sending your name, address, zip or postal code, along with a check or money order for $3.25 (please do not send cash), plus 75¢ postage and handling ($1.00 in Canada), payable to Silhouette Reader Service to:

In the U.S.	In Canada
3010 Walden Ave.	P.O. Box 609
P.O. Box 1396	Fort Erie, Ontario
Buffalo, NY 14269-1396	L2A 5X3

Please specify book title with your order.
Canadian residents add applicable federal and provincial taxes.

MARSH-3

Silhouette Books®

Take 4 bestselling love stories FREE

Plus get a FREE surprise gift!

Coming Soon

Fashion A Whole New You.
Win a sensual adventurous
trip for two to Hawaii via
American Airlines®, a
brand-new Ford Explorer
4 × 4 and a $2,000
Fashion Allowance.

Plus, special free gifts* are yours to
Fashion A Whole New You.

From September through November, you can take part in
this exciting opportunity from Silhouette.

Watch for details in September.

* with proofs-of-purchase, plus postage and handling

SLFW-TS